CRAVING CHARLESIA

PJ FIALA

RT
ROLLING
THUNDER

COPYRIGHT

1. Romance—Fiction. 2. Romance—Suspense. 3. Romance
- Military

I. Title – Craving Charlesia

ISBN: 978-1-942618-60-7

DEDICATION

I've had so many wonderful people come into my life and I want you all to know how much I appreciate it. From each and every reader who takes the time out of their day to read my stories and leave reviews, thank you.
My beautiful, smart and fun Road Queens, who play games with me, post fun memes, keep the conversation rolling and help me create these captivating characters, places, businesses and more. Thank you ladies for your ideas, support and love. The following characters and places were created by:

Charlesia Sampson - Belinda Jackson Hercule

Detective Samuel Bowers - Nicky Ortiz

Haylie Tomms - Cindy Pearson

W. Smith Cigar and Tobacco - Yvette Johnvin

Loretta Smith - Elinda Moody

Phillip Smith - April Shindlebower Brown

Richie Reynolds - Karen Cranford LeBeau

L.S. Mercantile - TeeAnn Kemmitz

Eleese - Tammy Jo Walker Ogren

Solveigh Janssen - Nathalie Juergensen

Saginaw Village - Ronda Barnes-Howard

Paxton - Kim Kurtz

Officer Eydie Evans (pronounced Eddi) - Eydie - Marlene Davis and Evans - Marie Evans

Nuthin' Fancy - Nancy Hoch

Randy Delhart - Melissa Hultz

Nick Scott - Denise Scott

Blue Zeus and Huckleberry - Jo Eddy

Jerard Maddox - Jerard (Terra Oenning) Maddox (Lynne Kerr)

Lucifer's Den - Lisa Webber

Las Vegas Sinners - Gene Fiala

Harvey Bowers (Dana Zamora) and Rebecca Bowers (Kristi Hombs Kopydlowski)

A very special thank you to April Bennett and Judy Rosen my amazing editors!

This gorgeous cover was designed by Stacy Garcia, Graphics by Stacy.

Photo image on the cover purchased from Eric McKinney at 612 Photograhy.

Last but not least, my family for the love and sacrifices they have made and continue to make to help me achieve this dream, especially my husband and best friend, Gene. Words can never express how much you mean to me. To our veterans and current serving members of our armed forces, police and fire departments, thank you ladies and gentlemen for your hard work and sacrifices; it's with gratitude and thankfulness that I mention you in this forward.

BLURB

Read the prequel to RAPTOR - RAPTOR Rising here.

A female operative with a point to prove.

A seasoned cop with a case to solve.

And the passion that ignites...

RAPTOR operative Charlesia Sampson is no damsel in distress. Surviving an explosion in the Army gave her more grit than glory, and now she'll destroy anyone who tries to hold her back. Dangerous missions are her forte. But when she's found at a murder scene, everything changes.

Finding Charly at the murder scene was difficult for Sam Bowers. But when the truth comes to light, Sam sees Charly differently. Together, they're determined to uncover the murderer and find a missing child--all while denying their need for one another.

One thing is certain: the sexy detective is CRAVING CHARLESIA.

***

Let's stay in contact, join my newsletter so I can let you know about new releases, sales, promotions and more. https://www.subscribepage.com/pjfialafm

1

Charly pulled up to the blue and white house she was watching on Jefferson Street. RAPTOR intel told them a kidnapper they were trying to locate had been seen entering the house about an hour ago. Currently, she was acting as if she was just another passerby, walking, but she was watching everything.

The houses on the street were not overly close together and most of them had large boxwood hedges between them. The large green hedges broke up the view and made it more difficult to keep an eye out down the street, so she'd have to get close and stay close.

As she approached the house next door, a yellow and white Cape Cod style house, she noticed the upstairs windows of her target house, the white house with the blue shutters, had a boarded-up window in the upstairs. Grimacing, she continued assessing the house from the sidewalk. She slowly walked past the house, keeping her eyes alert but not so much so that she would raise any attention. A little red wagon outside caught her attention, though it held potted plants and not toys. The two steps leading up to a small front porch were wooden and in need of paint but otherwise looked safe to walk on, though the front of the house sure didn't look like anyone used that entrance due to the cobwebs at the corners of the support posts and layer of dirt on the windows.

Charly bent and pretended to tie her shoe as she listened for any sounds.

A male voice yelled, "No."

At the same time the sound of a gun firing and the flash of light in the front window had Charly jumping up from her stooped position.

She quietly walked up the driveway to the back of the house, while she pulled her cell phone from her back pocket and tapped her icon to call in to RAPTOR.

"Piper here."

"Piper, I need back up here. A gun just went off in the house. I'm walking to the back to see if I can get inside."

"Charly, wait for assistance. Diego and Falcon are here, Creed is out but I'll call him."

"I can't wait. Just send them over right away. Thanks Pipes."

Pocketing her phone, Charly found the back door area had a small covered patio over the door and two steps to it. She plastered herself to the wall and listened for any sound but heard nothing. Slowly edging against the wall to the back door, she reached her right hand over and slowly twisted the knob. Relieved it turned, she gave the door a push and held her breath in case it made noise. Amazingly, it pushed open easily and she entered the house. The smell of gun powder was the first thing she noticed. The kitchen area was fairly clean, though there were some dirty dishes in the sink and a dirty bowl on the counter with a spoon in it.

The kitchen table was littered with newspapers and she saw a large dog crate to the right of the table with a blanket, pillow and a bottle of water in it. Her brow furrowed as she looked at the crate and her heart sank as she realized it likely wasn't for a dog at all.

Charly heard soft crying from a room beyond the kitchen; it sounded like a child. She edged her way to the door and peered around it into the next room which was the living room. Her heart sank as she took in the body of a grown man sprawled on the floor, and a young boy with red hair sitting on the floor. Not wanting to get shot herself, Charly inhaled and slowly let it out before saying, "Hey. Can I help you?"

The little boy looked up at her and Charly noticed that he still held the gun in his hands. She put her hands up in the air. "I won't hurt you. I heard the gun go off and wondered if you needed help."

The boy simply stared at her, then his eyes went to her left hand, which was a prosthetic from the elbow down. It was fashioned after a human forearm and hand, and had a skin-like covering over it. Four fingers and a thumb, though they didn't move like a human hand; it was a bit clumsy to use, though Charly was proud of how well she'd adjusted to it.

"I was a soldier in the army and lost my arm when we were in a bad accident."

She slowly turned her hand back and forth, then moved the fingers to show him how it worked.

The dazed boy stared and she took a couple more steps closer to him. "Do you need help? When I lost my arm, I needed help."

That blank stare continued and Charly crept slowly toward him. She stepped to the left, toward the boy avoiding the dead man lying on the floor, his blank eyes staring at the ceiling; his dark blue shirt was neat except for the small bullet hole right where his heart had likely stopped beating.

She looked at the boy again, then saw the sofa behind the boy and the chain laying on the floor, still tied to the leg of the sofa. She bit her bottom lip and studied him, noticing marks on his right ankle, no socks on his feet and dirty clothes on his body. The dark blue pants he wore were stained and the knees torn, the green and white striped shirt was filthy and wrinkled. His hair was chopped off haphazardly and as she looked closer, she noticed that his brows were brown, not red, and she suspected his hair had been dyed.

It was his brown eyes, however, that made her heart hurt. They were haunted and looked so familiar, but she couldn't quite place them.

"Honey, can I take the gun from you so neither of us gets hurt?"

Once she was a few steps away, she slowly lowered herself to the floor and sat down, then scooted herself toward him. Her prosthetic hand clumped when she dropped it to the floor and the boy looked down at it. She was slightly relieved that he made no movement.

"It's a bit heavy sometimes." Charly reassured him.

As she sat alongside him, she slowly reached over with her right hand and wrapped it around the stock of the pistol the boy held.

"May I take this, honey?"

The boy jerked and the gun went off again, landing another bullet into the man on the floor directly across from them. It confirmed that he was dead; he never moved an inch.

Taking the gun more firmly in her right hand, she wiggled it from his grip, trying to soothe him as she spoke, "It's alright honey, I'll help you out."

Someone entered the kitchen from the back and Charly sighed as her teammates arrived. Looking at the doorway, surprised wasn't even a good enough word for what she felt, when she saw none other than Detective Samuel Bowers standing in the doorway staring at her.

2

S am took in the situation, holding her attention for longer than strictly necessary.

"What happened here?"

Charly stared back, her lips pressed tightly together, her eyes wide—in fear or surprise? He couldn't tell. The little boy sitting on the floor next to her was spattered with blood and gazed straight ahead, unmoving. Sam had to look closely to see if he was even breathing.

"Charly? What happened?"

Charly looked at the little boy next to her then at the body of the man across the floor. When she looked back at him, her voice was quiet and unusually compliant. "There's been a horrible occurrence here."

"A horrible...an occurrence? Are you serious?"

"It's not what it looks like."

"Tell me what it is, Charly."

His chest constricted and indecision wrapped itself around him. She still held the gun and didn't seem herself, and he was reluctant to take another step into the room for fear of being shot.

"I um…" Charly looked at the little boy who finally moved and gaped up at her with such pitiful eyes it almost broke his heart. Charly's head leaned to the right as she assessed the little guy, then she took a deep breath and looked at him.

"So, this is complicated, Sam."

"Charly, honey, can you please put the gun down?"

She swallowed and looked down at the gun still in her hand. She seemed mesmerized and spent more time than Sam was comfortable with, staring at it. By this time, he was ready to walk out and wait for back up.

"Charly, don't make me pull my gun on you."

That seemed to jerk her to her senses. Her brow furrowed as she looked into his eyes. "Why would you pull your gun on me?"

He nodded to her hand, "You have a gun in your hand, one that has just been fired. The smell of gunpowder fills the room. I don't doubt you have GSR on your hands."

At the sound of footsteps behind him, Sam stepped back and dared a glance at the people coming into the house. Expecting to see his partner, he instead saw Diego Josephs and Falcon Montgomery.

Diego looked at him and nodded, then slowly walked to Charly and knelt down beside her.

"Can you drop the gun on the floor, Charly, so Sam can take it?"

Charly nodded at Diego, then slowly lay the pistol on the floor and pushed it away from her. Diego held out his hand toward Sam, who pulled a rubber glove from his back pocket and lay it in Diego's palm.

Using the glove to avoid leaving fingerprints on the gun, Diego picked it up and Sam held out a plastic bag for him to drop it into.

Securing the zip top on the bag, Sam watched as Diego then softly talked to Charly.

"Hey, it's all okay. Can you tell me what happened here?"

Charly looked at him, and then to Diego, and swallowed. "This little guy shot him." She lifted her right hand and pointed to the dead man on the floor a few feet away. "He was protecting himself. He was protecting himself." She repeated her words a few times and Diego softly rubbed her shoulder. "It's okay, Charly. We'll take care of both of you."

She nodded and angrily swiped at the tear that started to fall from the corner of her eye.

"We have to protect him, too."

She pointed to the scared little boy next to her who had further scooted into Charly's side. She looked down at him and whispered, "Do you want me to sit with you while you talk to Sam?"

The little boy nodded slightly; it was barely noticeable but Sam was watching closely, still not sure what was happening here.

Falcon stepped forward slightly, "Is that alright, Sam, if Charly stays with him?"

He nodded, what more could he do at that point? "Yes, I think that will be fine."

Sam stepped forward, "Charly, I need to take you both into the station."

"Why?" Her brow furrowed. "Why can't we talk here?"

"Honey, there's a body right across from you and the scene will need to be processed. I can bend the rules a bit here, but I don't have carte blanche to bend them all. Not even for you."

When she looked up at him a myriad of things happened inside at once. His heartbeat increased as he stared into those gorgeous blue eyes he'd been dreaming about late at night. His breathing constricted at the sadness that dimmed her normally bright eyes, and his mind screamed, "Wrap her in your arms and don't let go."

Forcing himself to ignore all of that, he looked at Diego, then turned to Falcon. "Can you two help Charly and this little guy out of the room? Please don't talk to her about this right now; I'm going to get my nuts in a wringer as it is."

Falcon stepped forward first and kneeled in front of the little boy, blocking his view from the dead man he'd been staring at. As soon as he blocked that view, the little boy focused on him. If you could see words being spoken, that look said it all. He was beseeching Falcon for help.

Falcon, so much like his father, Ford—strong, silent, independent, but always dependable—held his hand out to the little boy. After a few moments, the little boy took Falcon's hand in his and stood up slowly.

Falcon then stood, too. "Do you want me to carry you outside or do you want to walk?"

As soft as a feather floating on a breeze, the little guy said, "Carry."

Falcon nodded and lifted the boy up, keeping his back to the man on the floor, and without another word he walked out the back door.

Sam then watched Diego help Charly to her feet. She then took a deep breath and stared at him for a long time. He couldn't feel what she was trying to convey and he felt sad about that, but he didn't break eye contact with her, either. He nodded to her. "I'll take you both to the station and you can sit with him while we question him. I've got to get a social worker there first so it might be a while."

Charly's lips quivered. "Can you call Hadleigh?"

He nodded at Charly. "Sure. I can call Hadleigh."

3

She sat in the back of Sam's car, which wasn't a police cruiser but his own vehicle, and she wondered why he'd responded to a police call. He was a detective and usually not the first responder. She remembered that the little boy next to her looked so familiar and glanced down at him, huddled so quietly next to her. He stared straight ahead but then she saw his jaw move as if he was ready to say something. She waited though, wanting him to be ready without pummeling him with questions.

Slowly, his head turned to her. "You saved me before, but it didn't work."

"What?" Her brows bunched together and she studied his face. It was smudged with dirt and there were tracks where tears had once fallen, then been swiped away. "When did I save you before?"

He took a deep breath. "In the jungle."

In the jungle? She thought about the times she'd been in the jungle and the only time that came to mind was when she, Emmy, Diego, Van, and Creed had quit their jobs with Operation Live Again and RAPTOR had begun, unofficially. They'd saved three kids that day: James Sulpulveda, Damien Hafeman and...

"Oh my God, you're Olive Tomms."

Olive turned to her then, her eyes just as haunted as earlier and Charly touched her hair. Her pretty hair had been carelessly chopped off and dyed red in an effort to hide her identity.

"How in the hell are you in this situation again, Olive? What happened?"

"My mom needed money."

"She sold..."

The car door opened and Sam slid into the driver's seat, and Olive turned straight ahead and stopped speaking. Charly, sitting directly behind Sam, took a few deep breaths, partly to calm herself down and partly to keep herself from crying for all this little girl had been through. Everyone in her life had let her down, including Charly. She'd handed Olive over to child services expecting that she'd be taken care of, only to have them send Olive back to a mom who'd started her bullshit all over again. How did a system that was supposed to protect kids become their worst enemies?

"Charly?"

She looked up into the mirror and saw Sam watching her. "It'll be alright."

She gazed into his eyes. They were as unusual as he was. His left eye was green and his right eye was blue. But both eyes held a look of concern in them and, for the first time when she was in his presence, Charly wasn't smitten or giddy like a teenager, but honestly felt sad. She nodded but said nothing, afraid she'd break down crying and Olive didn't need that right now. She needed stability and strength, and she'd give that to her.

Sam closed his door and started the vehicle while Charly quietly reached over to take Olive's hand as they silently rode in the back of Sam's vehicle to the police station.

During the ride, Charly could feel Sam's eyes on her but she never looked at him. She simply watched the town pass by her window as she tried to formulate questions to ask no one in particular about what happens to these kids they work so hard to protect. The other two kids they'd rescued from the jungle had actually been kidnapped and returned to their families. But she wondered if anyone ever checked up on them to make sure they weren't in families like Olive's, and that they were getting the proper counseling they needed. She'd have to remember to ask Hadleigh about how these kids are handled within the framework of social services. The questions bombarded her brain and she felt the start of a massive headache at the base of her skull.

Sam pulled into the parking area of the police department and Olive squeezed her hand. Charly squeezed back, letting Olive know she was still there for her. At least, she hoped that's what she conveyed.

Sam quickly exited the vehicle and within just a second or two, opened her door and waited. When she didn't move right away, he held his hand out to her. She lifted her left arm, then hesitated because it wasn't real and she didn't know how he felt about it. Or her. She had been reluctant to admit that she had a crush on him. Hell, every woman who met him had a crush on him. He was imposing in size —she'd heard six foot nine inches, but not from him. His shoulders were broad and they narrowed slightly to his waist, though he still carried a fair amount of bulk. She could tell the man worked out.

He reached into the vehicle and took her left hand, and gave it a slight tug. "Come on, Charly. You think I don't know who you are?"

Her eyes locked on his then and while she waited for him to smile, he didn't, he just stared at her as if he were daring her to deny his words.

She turned her body and exited his SUV then held her hand inside for Olive. Olive took her hand and scooted across the seat, then hopped out of the vehicle, gripping Charly's hand tightly.

Charly leaned down slightly and whispered to Olive only, "I won't let them take you back home. I'll fight until I die before I let that happen to you."

Olive looked up at her and her sad brown eyes filled with moisture before one lone tear escaped and tracked its way down her dirty little face and plopped onto her soiled shirt. Charly's eyes then watered because, honest to God, that was the saddest little girl she had ever seen in her life and Charly was determined to let her know that not everyone in the world cared so little about kids. She cared. Charlesia Sampson cared deeply and wholeheartedly.

"Okay, let's get inside." Sam tugged Charly's left hand and Charly squeezed Olive's left hand and they walked into the police station all connected.

4

Sam took Charly and the child to an interrogation room and had them each sitting at the table. They were at a forty-five-degree angle to each other and he'd noticed that Charly barely let go of his hand the whole time. He was right about her; she had a big heart.

Once they'd been seated, he asked, "Do you want some water? How about something to eat?" His eyes landed on the little boy and held. "Do you need something to eat, buddy?"

Charly smiled for the first time in a while and looked at the child. "Olive, do you want a meal bar like you had on the plane? I can ask Diego to bring some."

Olive? It was a little girl? Charly had gotten that out of her? Charly then looked up at him and his heart swelled. "Sam, can you please ask Diego to bring Olive some jungle bars and a root beer?"

For the first time Olive smiled at Charly and Charly smiled back. "See, I remember."

Sam stood silently for a few moments trying to puzzle it all together but he was certain he was missing important information. "How about you Charly, do you want something?"

When her eyes landed on his, he saw hers dart back and forth between his and he felt embarrassed. It had been the topic of many bullying sessions when he was in grade school. "Sam two eyes", "Sam who can't decide what color his eyes should be." On and on. Once he'd started growing in high school, the taunts slowed down unless the opposing football team wanted to irritate him. But they found out quickly that it was a stupid mistake to taunt him. He'd ram them into the ground just for the fun of it afterwards; one time he even made a guy cry. He'd gone back to the bench and smiled as their coach called a time-out and pulled him aside asking what he was thinking.

"I was thinking that'll be the last time he calls me a weirdo."

His coach hung his head for a moment and Sam braced for a tirade, only to catch his coach smiling, then clearing his throat and saying, "You can't do that Sam. Unnecessary roughness will get us fouled."

"Yes, Coach," was all he said. But the truth of it was, that team didn't taunt him ever again. Oh, and they won that game 48 to 6.

Charly smiled softly. "I'll have what Olive is having."

Sam nodded and left the room. He walked down the hall to his office as he dialed Diego's number and waited for him to pick up.

"Josephs."

"Hey, Diego, Charly and Olive want jungle bars and root beer. She said you'd know what that means."

"Olive?"

"Yes, Olive. I don't know who Olive is but Charly seems to."

Diego sounded frustrated on the other end of the phone. "Olive Tomms?"

"I haven't gotten that far yet."

"Well, son of a bitch. I'll be right over."

"Thanks. I hope you'll be willing to fill me in on jungle bars and Olive Tomms."

"I'll do my best."

The line went dead and Sam waited a few moments to get his head on straight before making his way back to the interrogation room. He stopped in the kitchen and pulled three bottles of water from the fridge; that could be a beginning for them until Diego and Hadleigh got there.

When he entered the room both Charly and Olive looked up at him and waited.

"So, Diego is bringing jungle bars and root beer and assured me they won't smell the place up."

Olive smiled and Charly giggled. "They're simply meal bars and nothing gross. It's just our nickname for them."

"Okay. That's what he said when I asked."

Charly smiled then but he noticed they still held hands and his heart melted a little at the care Charly took with the little girl. He set the water bottles in front of each of them. "This is until Diego gets here. I didn't know if you were thirsty."

Charly nodded. "I am." She squeezed Olive's hand before letting go, then pulled her water bottle from the table. Tucking it between her left arm and her body, she twisted the cap off. She set that one in front of Olive, then did the same with the other. He felt bad for not offering but also knew she'd balk if he treated her like she was incapable. He knew that much about her and he admired her for it all the more.

Both Charly and Olive took drinks of their water. He followed suit, opened his water and took a long drink from it. A soft knock on the door sounded and he stood and opened it. Hadleigh Keach stood on the other side with a file in her hands and a smile on her face.

"Hi Sam, I was told Charly is in here with Olive Tomms."

He stepped back and let her in. He pointed to a chair to Olive's right and motioned for Hadleigh to sit down. Hadleigh reached across the table to Charly and Charly lay her left hand in Hadleigh's.

"Are you okay, Charly?"

"I'm fine. Hadleigh, this is Olive. Olive, this is my friend and Donovan's wife, Hadleigh. Do you remember Van?"

Olive's eyes rounded as she stared at Charly, then she nodded and turned to look at Hadleigh. "You're pretty."

"Thank you, Olive. You know Van?"

Olive nodded. "He saved me with Charly."

Sam sat to Charly's left and directly across the square table from Olive and merely watched. Hadleigh smiled at her. "They're pretty great, aren't they? So you must also know Diego, Emmy, and Creed?"

Olive nodded, a small smile on her face. Hadleigh set her bag on the floor and fished in it for a moment, pulling out some wet wipes. Sam sat forward, "We still have to take GSR tests. I have a technician coming in soon to do that, then you can wash up. I'm sorry."

Charly took Olive's hand once again. "It's alright, we'll wait."

Hadleigh made conversation while they waited. "Olive, how old are you?"

Olive swallowed and softly said, "Nine. I think."

The door opened and a technician walked into the room with a little kit. She quickly set her kit on the table and said, "I'm Jan and I'll be doing some quick swabs and tests. It won't hurt, I promise."

She quickly did her tests then Hadleigh slid the wet wipes toward Charly, who pulled a couple out of the package and handed one to Olive.

"This will make us feel better." She then wiped her hands off and Olive mimicked her. Then Charly leaned forward. "Can I help you wipe your face off?"

Olive nodded and Charly gently wiped the dirt and grime from Olive's face. "When we're finished here, we'll get ourselves a nice hot shower. Deal?"

"Deal." Olive softly replied.

5

It had taken some doing. Actually, it had taken a lot of doing, but Hadleigh, Emmy, as the leader of RAPTOR, and Sam had talked social services into letting Olive go home with Charly for the time being. Sam was so sweet after acting like he was all business. As soon as he found out about the lack of follow-up and support from social services for the Tomms girl previously, he jumped right in to help out. Charly's heart swelled.

Charly took Olive to her bathroom and turned the water on, getting the temperature just right.

"Okay, shampoo is here; it smells like oranges." She pointed to the bottles on the shelf in the shower. "This is the conditioner; it smells like oranges too. This is the shower soap; it just smells clean. You wash up and stay in here as long as you want. When you get out, I have a towel right here," she pulled the towel from the cabinet and set it on the stool across from the shower. "In the meantime, I'll be rounding you up some clothes to wear. Shelby and Diego have two kids..." She saw Olive's eyes get big. "They aren't babies. Diego met Shelby and her niece and nephew while on a mission. I think they're close in age to you. Callie is seven and Anders is five. When Shelby and Diego got married, they adopted Callie and Anders as their own children. I'm sure they have clothes you can wear until we get you some tomorrow. Deal?"

"Deal."

Charly winked at Olive and left the room so she had privacy; she'd likely had very little privacy in the past. Her heart ached for all this little girl had gone through and she was going to do her darnedest to make sure from this point forward, her life was the best life it could be. Though she didn't know how she was going to do that, or what parameters she could work within. But she was going to help Olive out.

She walked out to her living room and called Shelby. They were still living upstairs so it shouldn't take too long to get some clothes for Olive.

"Hey Shelby, not sure if Diego explained what's going on here, but do you have a couple outfits Olive can wear until I can take her shopping for her own clothes? Maybe a pair of pajamas too?"

"Sure. Diego mentioned you brought her home and some of what's gone on. I'll bring down some larger sizes and some other things she may need."

"Thank you. Thank Callie too."

"It's our pleasure. I'll be right down with the clothes."

Hanging up, she sat and stared across the room at nothing in particular. Her phone rang and she quickly picked it up without looking at who was on the other end.

"Charly here."

A low, deep-throated chuckle sent goose bumps up her arms and down her legs. "It's Sam. How are things going?"

"Good. Good. Things are good." She nervously chattered.

He chuckled. "Okay. I just thought I'd check. And, I wanted to let you know that..." He paused and her heart beat so rapidly she thought it would run right out of her chest. "I'm proud of you for today."

Tears sprang instantly to her eyes and she swiped at them almost angrily. "Proud?"

"Yeah." He took a deep breath and she longed to see his face. "Look, Charly, I know we've danced around this for a few months now. And, honestly, I don't know why I've hesitated to ask, but I think it's because I thought you'd say no. But, will you go...do you want to go out? To dinner? Or something? Maybe a drink. Oh, that is, if you drink. I mean you don't have to, you could have a soda or something." She heard him mumble, "Shit."

"Yes." Her stomach summersaulted and she wrapped her left arm around it while she sat forward just a bit. "Yeah, I'd like to go out to dinner or a drink or something, but this really is an awkward time."

"Really?"

"Yeah. Really."

She could hear him let out a long breath, then clear his throat. "Okay. That's awesome. I know you have Olive now and it's awkward, but in a couple of weeks? We don't have to stay out long. I just, well, honestly I think it's time we sit down and get to know each other a bit better."

She giggled. "I do too. Thank you, Sam. For breaking the ice, I mean. Let's talk about this in a couple of weeks."

A soft knock on her door sounded and she stood. "Hey, I don't mean to cut you off, but Shelby is at my door bringing some clothes for Olive to wear. Do you mind if I end this call now?"

"Of course not. Take care of Olive and we'll see each other soon. I'll call you Saturday and we'll figure it all out."

"Sounds good. Thanks, Sam."

"Good night, Charly."

She wanted to sit and bask in the sound of his voice for a while longer. But instead, she opened the door for Shelby.

"Hi, I brought a bunch of things down and separated them out for you."

Charly sighed. "Come in. Olive is still in the shower."

"Okay." Shelby walked to the sofa and laid out two piles of clothes.

"This pile here are clothes that Callie and Anders can't wear. If any of these clothes fit Olive, she can have them. I needed to clean out their drawers for a while now and this is the perfect time. I know Callie is younger than Olive, but Diego said she was very small. This pile here Callie still wears but she has plenty to wear in the meantime.

Use what you can. I also have a couple pairs of underwear for her."

"Thank you so much Shelby. These are fantastic."

Charly picked up some of the cute shirts Callie couldn't wear and thought they'd likely fit. Olive was so small right now, mostly due to lack of nutrition. And while Callie didn't always have it easy, she was tall for her age.

The shower turned off and Charly heard the shower door open and close.

Shelby smiled. "I'll get out of here so she isn't startled. I assume we'll meet her at breakfast."

"Yeah, I'll bring her down in the morning."

Shelby nodded and quickly left Charly's apartment at about the same time the bathroom door opened. Charly made her way to her bedroom, which was also where the bathroom was located.

"Hi, Olive. Stay there, I've got some awesome clothes for you. Shelby just dropped them off. I'll bring them in. Hang tight."

Charly held up a couple of shirts for Olive to see. Olive smiled and her eyes looked brighter. Her clean little face was so sweet. Charly could see the little girl she remembered emerging. Some of the red even faded from her hair, which was good. Maybe it was a temporary color. She'd take her to the salon tomorrow to get a proper haircut and see about that color coming out. That would make Olive feel so much better.

6

S am entered the police station and meandered toward his office. That was a term they each used loosely, as the rooms were small and it was a no-frills department. But they got the job done. Too bad he didn't feel that right now.

Plopping down in his desk chair, Sam switched his monitor on and shook the mouse to wake up the computer. The first email he saw was from their captain, Jason Peters. He opened the email and began reading. His blood ran colder the further into the report he read.

"Hey Sam, good work yesterday."

Sam looked up to see Rory Richards standing in his door-way. "Was it? Rory, what the hell is going on here? We live in a small town and in the past couple of years we've dealt with jewel thieves, child pornographers, and now traffick-ing? What the fuck?"

Rory let out a heavy sigh. "I know it seems like it shouldn't be here and so much of it, but we're not really any different than any other town or city. It just seems like it shouldn't be here because we're small, and it impacts us more because we know so many of the locals, where in a large city we don't. But crime is everywhere, buddy."

"Yeah." Sam sat back in his chair and sighed.

"Chin up, Sam, I hear Captain has been given the okay to hire RAPTOR. They're good and since they're on the case, we should have high hopes the trafficking ring will be stopped."

"I agree with you there. I'm reading the captain's report right now. Olive Tomms has a sister, Haylie, who was sold at the same time as Olive. That's how the captain got permission to hire RAPTOR."

"You've got to be kidding me."

"Apparently, that's why Olive shot Harry Smith, her captor. He had the girls together but then brought Olive to the house he was killed in. She wanted to be with her sister again."

"Do you know where the sister is?"

"Not yet. Charly and RAPTOR are trying to figure it out. Captain called Emmy at RAPTOR to work on the details of the hiring and told her about Haylie."

Rory whistled and shook his head. He cleared his throat and rotated his shoulders to loosen the tension creeping in. Changing the topic, he ventured, "So, I understand you had to go round and round yesterday with social services."

"Well, Hadleigh Keach navigated most of the deep waters for us. She knew just what buttons to push and the right words to say. Given the system has let these little girls down before, and there wasn't a case worker assigned to their case, especially after she'd been returned from traffickers more than a year ago, what could they say? Hadleigh tightened the screws pretty hard on them and made the director seem rather embarrassed at the lack of follow-up. Given RAPTOR's training and Hadleigh's social work background, it was hard to argue there was a better place for Olive. But I don't doubt, to save face, the Department of Health and Human Services will try again at some point to pull Olive out of Charly's care. We'll have to see."

"Where's Olive's mom?"

"She's a druggy. Needed money and sold Olive and Haylie to get a fix or two. We're looking for her now, but it seems she's in the wind."

"How about the father?"

"He's no better. And at this point, we don't know who he is."

"Christ, it irritates me when people like Alice and me struggle to have kids and then losers like that have them and abuse them."

Sam rubbed the back of his neck. "I agree."

"By the way, we haven't told anyone else, but Al is finally pregnant."

"No kidding? Congratulations, man." Sam stood and walked around his desk and hugged his friend.

"Thanks. If we can just get past Al's puking constantly, all will be good."

Sam grimaced. "Yikes."

"Yeah, but we've been trying for a while now and Alice was afraid she was too old to get pregnant, so she's not complaining. Much."

Sam stepped back. "I'm happy for you both."

Rory took a deep breath. "Thanks. Okay. Keep me in the loop and if you need anything, let me know."

"Will do Rory, thanks."

Sam inhaled and sat at his desk to finish reading the report from their captain. Most of what he read made his stomach turn.

A knock on his door frame had him turning to see his captain standing in his doorway.

"Hey, Cap, come on in. I just finished the report you wrote up from yesterday's findings. Do we have anything on Harry Smith?"

"Not yet. So, the investigation as to the Tomms girls is up to RAPTOR, but we still have some work to do as to Smith and some of his criminal activities. Not only is he a trafficker, but we found a plethora of guns in his house. A plethora meaning there were more than forty. We need to check registrations on all of them and if they aren't his, find out who they are registered to and how he got them."

"Okay. Is that where you want me to start?"

"Right now, the guns and other evidence gathered from the house is downstairs in the evidence room. Go through it and see if there's enough evidence to get a search warrant for his bank accounts and credit card statements. We're also looking for unusual purchases and, even though it's always a crap shoot, see about cell phone records."

"You've got it, Cap. I'll see what I can do."

"Why don't you see if Charly will let you talk to Olive Tomms? Find out how she got the gun and if she has any information, even though it may not seem like much."

"Okay. I spoke to Charly a little bit ago and she's taking Olive to have her hair cut today and then to see a counselor."

"Okay. Well, do what you can with the evidence and then deal with Charly and Olive later."

"Yep." Sam hefted himself out of his office chair and walked to the kitchen for a cup of coffee before heading downstairs to slog through the evidence. After setting his coffee on the table in the evidence room, he pulled his phone out and dialed Charly.

"Hey, Sam, what's up?"

"Hi, Charly, I know you and Olive have a busy morning but I'd like to come by and talk to Olive at some point today. She may be able to tell us enough to help us figure out some of this stuff here. Is there a time that will work?"

She hesitated and Sam stiffened his spine. "Let me call you back after the meeting with the counselor. I want to see how she handles that."

7

Charly didn't want to put Sam off in that way, but Olive came first. Olive entered the living room, looking better rested, though Charly heard her tossing and turning last night.

"Olive, I noticed you didn't sleep well. Do you need a better mattress or bed?"

Olive shook her head but her solemn brown eyes never left Charly's.

Charly smiled, "Just all that's gone on?"

Olive nodded; so did Charly.

"I get it." Charly stood. "Ready to go down to breakfast?"

"Yeah."

Waiting at the door for Olive to join her, Charly took a deep breath. Today would be hard for Olive. Likely not as hard as some of her previous days, but hard just the same. As Olive neared her, Charly opened the door, and as she stepped into the hall, Charly held her right hand out for Olive to hold. She looked up at her and hesitated before moving to Charly's left, then took her left hand, which had Charly's throat clogged with the biggest lump she'd ever had in there. She stared down at Olive as the moisture in her eyes had Olive's visage waving, but there was an understanding between them. They were both broken.

Taking a deep breath, she led Olive to the kitchen where the aromas filling the air made her stomach growl.

"I smell Sheldon's fresh cinnamon rolls. Wait till you have one of those. They are the best anywhere around, I guarantee it."

"I don't know what that is."

Charly's brows bunched together and for the third time that morning, her eyes glistened with moisture. Olive had never even had a cinnamon roll.

"Well, you're about to have the best ones in the world, so I guess that will ruin you for all other cinnamon rolls. Lucky you."

"Why is being ruined lucky?"

Thinking about her choice of words Charly grimaced. "It just means that any other cinnamon roll you eat won't be as good as the ones Sheldon makes. So, it's a figure of speech that means all others will fail in comparison."

"Okay." Olive's voice was very quiet then and Charly shook their clasped hands.

"Hey, are you sad?"

Olive began crying. "I thought you meant I was ruined. That I'm bad."

Charly stopped and knelt down in front of her. Pulling Olive into her arms she held her close, relieved when Olive wrapped her arms around Charly's shoulders.

Softly she explained while holding Olive, "I didn't mean that at all. You are not ruined or bad. If anything sweetie, you're saved. You're lucky in that from this point on, you have a whole team of people here that are going to work night and day to make sure your life is a good life. And we're going to find Haylie and make sure she has a good life too."

Olive clung to her for a long time and Charly let her. When Olive was ready to pull away, Charly looked into her eyes. Her lashes were spiked from the tears that pulled them together but most of the sadness from just a moment ago seemed to have dissipated.

Olive's stomach growled and Charly giggled. "I guess we'd better go eat."

Olive nodded.

"Are you alright Olive?" She held eye contact and searched for any signs of distress.

"Yeah."

"Okay." Charly stood, took Olive's hand in her left hand once again, and walked into the kitchen. Sheldon turned as they entered.

"Good morning. I heard we have a guest. Please introduce us, Charly."

"Sheldon, this is Olive. Olive, this is Sheldon, the best cook in all the land and the reason this room always smells like heaven."

Sheldon chuckled but looked at Olive. "It's nice to meet you, Olive. What are some of your favorite foods?"

Olive stared at Sheldon for a moment, then she shrugged. Sheldon nodded.

"That's good. That means I should be able to make all sorts of things and you'll try them. Then you can tell me what you liked best and what you didn't. Deal?"

Olive nodded. "Deal."

Charly smiled at Sheldon and he nodded. She walked Olive into the dining room where Diego, Shelby, Callie, and Anders were eating breakfast. She made the introductions and Callie got out of her chair and walked over to Olive.

"I'm glad you can wear that shirt. I was sad when I couldn't wear it anymore. It's cool isn't it?"

Olive nodded.

"Do you want to sit by me?"

Olive looked up at Charly. Smiling, Charly nodded. "I'll get you some things to eat if you want to sit down and I'll sit on the other side of you if that's okay."

Olive walked to the table with Callie and the girls sat down.

Charly smiled at Shelby and mouthed, "Thank you," and received a genuine smile in return. They'd purposely planned on being down here for Olive.

Filling two plates with fresh fruit and a cinnamon roll, Charly set the plates on the table and the look on Olive's face was both pleasing and heartbreaking. She'd likely never had a plate of food like this. Charly walked back to the buffet and filled two glasses, one with milk and one with orange juice and brought them to Olive. She couldn't even look at her this time, she was so close to breaking down and sobbing her eyes out at the lack in Olive's life. She walked once again to the buffet and took a deep breath and held it for a moment.

Diego came to stand beside her. "You okay?"

Charly nodded, afraid to open her mouth and say anything.

"It'll be like this for a while Charly. Remember our training and hold firm in the belief that we will make a difference for Olive and Haylie. Know it in your heart and know we are all here for you. For all of you."

"Than..." She stopped and cleared her throat lightly. "Thanks. You guys are the best."

Diego chuckled. "There are days that Callie and Anders will tell you differently."

8

Sam looked at the list of guns, serial numbers, calibers, and registered owners he'd spent the morning compiling. Rory had been good enough to come down and help him pull the list together or he'd still be there at midnight. Captain was right, all of the guns were registered to someone else. All were stolen, many not even reported stolen, which could mean the owners didn't know the guns were missing, or the owners were afraid to report that a gun had been stolen. Or, worst case scenario, the owners were dead. That was their next check.

His phone rang and he gladly set the offending list down on the table and pulled his phone from his pocket.

"Bowers."

"Hey Sam, it's Charly."

His stomach fluttered like the time he'd fallen in love with Janet Darrow in first grade. She'd looked at him with those blue eyes and smiled. She'd recently lost her front tooth but he remembered being so smitten with her. She told him she liked his two different-colored eyes. Most boys were average; Sam was special because of it. She'd asked him if he had magical powers and he'd said, "Yeah." He so wanted to impress Janet.

"Hey Charly."

"Ah, we're finished with the counselor and Olive thought she'd be able to sit and chat with you a bit. You're going to be nice to her aren't you?"

"What?" He shook his head. "Of course. I can't belie..." He pulled his shoulders back and took a deep breath. "You don't even have to ask that, Charlesia."

"I didn't mean to make you mad. I just have to be sure."

Sam squared his shoulders back and sighed. "I understand."

"Okay. We'll be at the station in about twenty minutes."

"Okay, Charly. See you then."

Sam ended the call and looked down the table at the ridiculous number of stolen guns they'd found. There was a stack of photographs at the end of the table showing where each weapon had been found. Luckily a couple of loose floorboards had caused a very good cop to look underneath and a huge stash had been found there.

"Unreal isn't it?"

Sam turned to see his captain entering the evidence room.

"That it is."

Sam rubbed his jaw and thought for a moment. "Captain,

I'd like to rent that infrared equipment from the Indiana State Police. The stuff that looks into walls and floors. We only lifted loose floorboards because we can't go in and rip up the place, but what if there are more guns in there? What if there's something else in there? And look at all these guns, but only two fifty-round boxes of 9mm shells were found. Where's all the ammo? Usually, these gun runners steal ammo with the guns. They make loads of money from the sale. They wouldn't leave it behind."

Captain looked down the table and thought about Sam's request. He inhaled deeply and stepped back from the table. "I'll check on cost and availability. Nice thinking on the ammo."

Sam watched the captain walk out the door and heard his footsteps fade on the metal stairs as he went up to his office.

Sam grabbed his notebook off the table and left the evidence room, locking the door behind him so things stayed as they were until he could get back down there.

Dropping his tablet on his desk, he left to use the restroom and wash his hands before Charly and Olive arrived. He felt a bit sheepish to be excited about seeing Charly again, but he also admitted to himself that he simply couldn't help it. He'd been crushing on her for a few months now.

Exiting the bathroom, he heard chattering at the front of the office and made his way up front expecting to see Charly and Olive. Instead, he saw the gorgeous red hair, that gleamed where the sun hit it from the windows, and Alice Richard's smile as she was congratulated by his fellow office mates. Alice Richards was former DEA, had worked in their department on special assignment, and been reunited with Rory after years of not seeing each other. Their relationship was interesting to watch re-blossom. It didn't take them long to get back together and finally, she was now expecting their first child. In her mid-forties, that was exciting news indeed.

Al looked up at him when he entered the room, the broad smile on her face was electric. Rory stood alongside Al, with a grin on his face that said it all. He was a man who had the world by the ass, that was for sure.

"Sam, it's so great to see you."

Al walked to him and he eagerly embraced her in a hug. "I understand congratulations are in order. I'm incredibly happy to hear the news. You two will be outstanding parents."

"Thank you, Sam. I'm over-the-moon happy. At least I will be once my mornings don't consist of me hovering over a toilet bowl."

Sam winced and Al laughed her usual bold laugh.

The door opened and there stood Charly. It was as if everyone else had faded into the background and a spotlight shone on her. Her short blonde hair was a riot of curls and the blue of her eyes looked almost electric. Her smile was perfection all by itself, but added to the total package that was Charlesia Sampson, it was breathtaking.

She looked directly at him and he felt like he was wearing cement shoes. She walked toward him, and his brain finally engaged and took in the whole scene. Olive walked alongside Charly, her hair now dark, cut into an adorable little pixie cut and shining under the florescent lights of the police station. She was clean, wore a cute little purple shirt with a unicorn on it, had color in her face and cheeks and looked like an entirely different little girl than she'd looked yesterday.

"Hi Sam." Charly greeted. Was she a little breathless?

"Hey Charly. Hi Olive."

"Hi," Olive replied quietly.

Sam took a deep breath, "Why don't we go into the conference room? It's nicer than an interrogation room, cleaner too, and will be more comfortable."

"Okay." Charly responded.

Sam held out his hand toward the conference room and waited as Charly and Olive walked past him. He stole a look, maybe two, probably more like three, at Charly's mighty fine ass and his cheeks heated.

9

Charly seated Olive in a chair and then sat to her right. Sam walked into the room and the first thing she smelled was his aftershave. Goose bumps rose on her arms and her nipples pebbled. She'd noticed his aftershave the first time she'd met him, a few months ago. They'd been at a crime scene, certainly not a romantic setting, but it was at a convenience store and Charly had been chasing a kid they suspected of helping a drug dealer get his friends stoned. Sam was responding to a call that the store had been robbed. She'd found herself glancing at him more than she should, but he was impressive. Tall, broad shoulders, and while his waist wasn't super trim, it narrowed to his spectacular hips. And, whew, he had some amazing thighs. His khakis had stretched over them when he bent down to retrieve a shell casing from the floor and she couldn't look away. Then a couple weeks later, she saw him playing baseball with his co-workers and he was wearing shorts. It was a casual goof-off day for them so no uniforms and oh was she happy about that. She sat on the bleachers that day with

Piper and found it difficult to look away from Sam as he played ball. He towered over everyone else. But he laughed easily with his friends, he was kind to others, and he was so damned handsome.

Sam looked over at them and asked, "Do you want a bottle of water or a soda?"

He was so thoughtful. She looked at Olive. "Do you need something Olive?"

Olive looked up at her, her eyes earnest, but when she spoke, it was soft and hard to hear. "Can I have a soda?"

Charly smiled at her. "What kind would you like?"

Olive simply shrugged.

Charly looked up at Sam. "What's your favorite soda, Sam?"

"I like Dr. Pepper. It's a cola with a hint of cherry flavoring in it."

Olive nodded and Sam smiled. "You got it. Charly, what about you?"

"I'll take a Dr. Pepper too."

Sam left the room and Olive turned to face her. "He likes you."

Charly's heart raced a bit but she cleared her throat. "That's nice. I like him too."

Olive nodded.

Sam entered the room with three Dr. Peppers and set them on the table. He opened the first one and handed it to Olive. Taking the second can in his hand, he opened that one up and gave it to her with a wink. That wink, oh goodness the things it did to her body.

She watched as he opened up the last can and took a long drink out of it. She looked at Olive who giggled then picked up her own soda can and took a sip.

"Mmm, that's good." She giggled.

Charly then took a drink of her soda and felt a bit of happiness for this little gal who was likely drinking her first Dr. Pepper because of her. Actually because of Sam, but either way, Olive was benefiting and that was nice.

Sam opened up the top of his leatherbound folio and pulled a pen from a pocket inside.

"Olive, I am simply trying to figure out where Harry Smith had all of his guns hidden. Do you know any special hiding places we can look to find them all? You'd really be helping me out."

Olive stared at Sam for a long time and Charly got the feeling she was waiting for Sam to fidget or move, which he didn't.

"He had some in the floor in the living room. He had some in the kitchen closet under the garbage. He had some in the room upstairs where he slept."

"Did he have bullets for the guns too?"

"At the other house."

"There's another house?"

Olive nodded. Charly sat up straighter and looked across the table at Sam. Swallowing, she slowly turned to face Olive. "Honey, do you know where the other house is?"

Olive shook her head. "It took a long time to get there."

"You were at the other house before?"

Olive nodded. "Haylie is there. I wanted to go back."

Charly leaned closer and took Olive's right hand in both of hers. "Can you think hard and tell me the name of the town or the street or did you see any numbers on the house? I want to find Haylie for you."

"N-4-3-0-9. I saw the number on a red sign at the end of the driveway when we left. I was crying and he yelled at me. But I saw the numbers. I remembered them so I could go back."

"Oh, Olive, that's a big help. Thank you." Charly leaned over and hugged her.

Sam then asked, "Olive, how did you get the gun you had yesterday?"

"He set it on the table to get a beer. He thought I was upstairs but I got out. I watched from the top of the steps. Then I went down to get it. I told him I wanted Haylie. He called me a brat. I pointed the gun at him and he yelled, 'No.' But I shot. I didn't mean to. It was heavy and I wanted to scare him."

"Okay. It's okay. You aren't in trouble for that Olive." Sam looked at her and smiled to help calm Olive. "Did he always have the gun out?"

Olive nodded. "He played with it."

Sam continued to write and ask his questions in a friendly manner. But Charly saw his jaw tighten and relax a few times. "Okay. Is there someone else at the other house?"

Nodding again, Olive said, "Tammy, Dante, and Haylie. We weren't supposed to talk but we did."

Charly squeezed Olive's hand. "It's okay to talk now Olive. You're helping us so we'll be able to find Tammy, Dante, and Haylie."

"I don't want Tammy." Olive's facial expression changed as she mentioned Tammy. Her brow furrowed and her bottom lip trembled.

"Oh, why don't you want Tammy?"

"She's bad. She's mean and yells all the time."

"Do you know Tammy's last name?"

"Smith. I heard Harry call her a bitch. He said, 'Tammy Smith the biggest bitch in the world.'"

Charly nodded and squeezed Olive's hand again. A quick glance at Sam and she noted he was writing it all down so she continued.

"Was Harry married to Tammy?"

Olive shrugged. "I don't think so. He said something about Junior being 'sponsible for Tammy."

"Okay, so maybe Harry Smith has a son. Junior, he called him. Did you ever see Junior?"

Olive shook her head. "Haylie did. She said he smells."

"I don't doubt it at all." Charly looked over at Sam and waited to see if he had more questions.

Sam smiled at Olive. "Do you remember what color the other house is, Olive?"

"Greenish." Sam wrote that down and while he still wrote he asked, "What color hair does Tammy have?"

"White." Olive shrugged. "But it's fake."

Sam looked up at Olive, a grin on his face. "Her hair is fake, like she wears a wig?"

"No, she has a dark stripe down her head."

Olive motioned with her fingers down the center of her head and Charly giggled.

"She dyes her hair blonde but she has dark roots?"

"Yeah. Harry said she's a whore."

10

S am tried not to smirk or grin but Olive, in her innocence, was rather funny.

"Olive, did Harry Smith go to the other house often?"

Olive looked at the tabletop for a few moments then looked up at Sam. "Just sometimes like once a week."

"What would he do when he went to the house?"

"Tammy would leave for a while. Harry said she was whoring around but was supposed to be working."

"What was her job?"

Sam glanced at Charly who remained still and continued to hold Olive's hand. He watched as Olive's thumb moved along the prosthetic thumb on Charly's left hand. He noticed Charly watching it too and he wondered about it.

"She was supposed to find more girls."

Charly took a drink of her soda and Sam noticed her hand shook slightly. He waited till she finished and was happy when she looked into his eyes. He held her gaze for a few seconds and he hoped he conveyed a strength and confidence in his because he wanted her to feel safe. Taking on Olive was going to be difficult. Olive would likely need a lot of counseling and retraining since her childhood so far had been anything but normal. Rules that kids followed such as a regular bedtime and bath time hadn't been part of Olive's upbringing. But also, behaviors that children who had been abused exhibited, such as acting out, lying to protect themselves, and more, would need to be worked through.

Taking a deep breath, Sam looked at Olive and lowered his voice to what he hoped was a softer tone.

"Olive, did Tammy find you and Haylie?"

Olive's lips trembled and her eyes filled with tears. She stared at her hand clasping Charly's while she tried to process her answer, or maybe his question.

Charly leaned over and kissed the top of Olive's head.

"It's alright, Olive. Sam and I only need the information so we can find Haylie and also stop these people from taking any more kids."

"But my mom didn't want me and Haylie. Those other kids' moms didn't want them. Where do they go if they don't go with Tammy?"

Charly turned in her chair and gently turned Olive's chair so they were face to face. "Your mom is sick. The drugs got hold of her. I'm sure it isn't that she didn't want you, but with the drugs in her, she doesn't know what she's doing. That doesn't make it right. It also doesn't mean you should have to live like that. Or Haylie. Or Dante. Or anyone else. That's my job, to stop that from happening and find people who want kids in their lives and will be good to them. None of that means you are bad. If anyone is bad, your mom is for getting started on the drugs in the first place."

Olive nodded slowly. "Tammy got Haylie first. Mom got money. I saw her get it. I was so scared when Haylie went away and I cried for a long time. Then my mom asked me if I'd be happier with Haylie and I said yes. So she called Tammy. Then Tammy came to get me and Mom got more money."

Sam watched Charly swallow repeatedly and he knew she was fighting her emotions. She pulled Olive to her for a hug and held her for a long time. Sam was about ready to climb right out of his skin. He wanted to find Tammy and kick the shit out of her, and Junior too. But first and foremost, he knew they were fighting against the clock because if they were paying for these kids, they would need to make money on them soon. That would come either through prostitution or selling them off to others who would do the same to them.

He sat back in his chair and worked at not clenching his jaw. Charly looked at him from behind Olive and their gazes held. She would be fierce at protecting Olive and Haylie if they could find her. There would be no one who would be a better protector for them than Charly. And, as much as he knew that it was selfish and immature to think this way, he felt like there would be no room in her life for him, and that made him terribly sad.

He softly cleared his throat, "I'll give you two a moment while I have someone start searching through the database for addresses with N4309 and a green house."

He stood and Charly pulled back and smiled at him. "Thank you, Sam."

His throat clogged so he didn't bother trying to say anything, he simply nodded and left the room.

He walked to Rory's office and saw him sitting at his computer, his brow furrowed.

"Hey, what's up?"

Rory turned, "Just looking over the evidence retrieved yesterday and trying to piece it all together."

Sam walked in and opened his folio, "I have something I need processed. Charly and Olive are in the conference room but I did get some information from Olive."

He turned his notes around so Rory could see them and watched as his friend read them.

"I'll start working on the address and names." He picked up his phone and snapped a picture of the notes, then emailed them to himself. "I got them."

Sam picked up his folio and turned to leave the room. "Thanks, Rory."

"Yep. Did Olive say why she was separated from Haylie?"

"I didn't get that far in the questioning. They needed a moment and I wanted to get started on searching while we finish up."

Rory nodded. "I get it."

Sam left and soon could hear Rory's keyboard keys clacking.

He walked back to see if Captain was in. The light in his office was on, so that was a good sign.

"Hey, Captain," he said as he stopped in the doorway.

"Hey. How did your interview go?"

"Still going. Did you have any luck locating any shipping companies coming into the area?"

"Not yet. Remember when the Santarinos were running their operation through town? I thought going back through the files, checking out if any of our suspects are connected to Rush Trucking, might help. Trouble is, after the old man was sent down for gunrunning, his kids split. They're nowhere around. Maybe the Smiths are using smaller trucks this time. But the economy around here hasn't picked up in the past couple of years and we might get lucky again. Maybe they're just shipping a couple of kids at a time."

"That's not a bad idea. What about U-Haul and other rental companies? They'd likely not use their own trucks for fear of being caught."

"Yeah. I'll check that, and rental car companies for any repeat rentals."

Sam nodded and left the captain's office to finish his interview with Olive. His heart felt heavier now than it did earlier.

11

D riving home from the interview with Sam, a thought popped into Charly's head.

"Hey, I have a good idea. I need new bedding. I've always wanted something shiny and pretty but haven't had the time to shop. Emmy is having a regular bed installed in my apartment today and you'll need new bedding too. How about we go shopping for sheets and comforters?"

Olive turned to look at her, but the look she gave Charly was unreadable.

"Do you mean my own bedspread and sheets? That I can keep?"

"Sure, why not?"

Olive shrugged.

Charly glanced quickly at her then back at the road. "Olive, I know things haven't always been good for you, but I promise, I'm trying very hard to make them good from this point on."

"I know."

"So, you and I, we need to have an agreement. Just between us. When you're feeling sad, scared or lonely, you need to let me know. The same if you're feeling over-whelmed. Then, you need to be honest with me and tell me what you need when that happens. Sometimes, it might be that you need some time alone. Sometimes you might need a hug. Sometimes you might want to talk. You need to tell me so I know how to handle it."

"Okay."

Charly took a deep breath. "Okay. Good. Now, what are you feeling about new bedding?"

"Yeah."

"Yeah? You want some? Really?"

Olive nodded and a smile lit up her face.

"Great. I know just the place."

Charly continued on to L.S. Mercantile, a small store in town; she'd seen the prettiest comforter set in the window a couple of weeks ago and vowed to find time to get it.

"Are we going to stay at your place?"

"Sure. At least until everything is final."

"What does final mean?"

"Well, it means many things. First, we need to find Haylie. Second, we need to figure out what's going to happen with your parents."

"I don't want to go there."

"I'm trying very hard to make sure you never have to again. Which means your parents will need to sign over custody. It shouldn't be hard since your mom took money for you. And this is the second time. It shouldn't have happened."

Olive nodded.

"Then, and this is the hardest part, we need to make sure you and Haylie are in a good and safe home where nothing bad will ever happen to you."

"Is that your home?"

Charly swallowed. She didn't want to lie and she did have reservations about the feasibility of having both girls with her and if authorities would allow it. She wasn't married. She had a dangerous job. She had to leave for work, sometimes for several days. Even though there were plenty of people available to take the girls on short notice while she was gone, getting Family Services to see that would be difficult. Plus, it wasn't likely the best situation for the girls. All that mattered at this time was that the girls were in a safe home. And consistency was needed to help them adjust.

"I think my home is safe. And I will do anything to make sure nothing happens to you. That said, sometimes I have to leave for work and be gone for long periods of time. Family Services will make a big deal out of that."

Olive turned and looked out the passenger window.

"I don't want to lie to you, Olive. But, Hadleigh, you met her yesterday, Donovan's wife, is a social worker and I'm going to talk to her about what we can do. We'll work hard to do what's best for you. And Haylie. Not what's best for me. You need to always remember that. What's best for you and Haylie is priority."

"Okay."

"Yeah?"

Charly pulled into the lot at L.S. Mercantile. She looked at Olive. "Is there anything you want to say or talk about before we go in and buy our bedding?"

"What's the point? You'll buy bedding and I might not be staying with you."

"You won't go anywhere you don't want to go and you can take your bedding with you if you do go somewhere."

"Really?"

"Of course."

Olive stared at her for a long time and Charly never looked away. She'd noticed that was Olive's way. She'd stare at a person for a long time, if she suspected they weren't telling the truth, to see if they fidgeted or seemed nervous. She'd told Olive the absolute truth. It was the most important thing she could do for her.

Once Olive was comfortable, she opened her car door and Charly did the same. They walked into the store together and Charly walked back to the linen department.

"I fell in love with a comforter I saw in the window and I hope it's still here."

Charly looked around the store and found the comforter she'd seen displayed, on a table.

"There it is."

She walked toward it, Olive right beside her. The two-toned gray silken comforter had a beautiful sheen that captured the light from the fluorescent lighting overhead. Charly smoothed the material with her right hand, enjoying the feel of it beneath her fingers.

"Feel how soft."

Olive felt the comforter and smiled. "It feels like baby skin."

"It does. But how do you know what baby skin feels like?"

Olive shrugged. "I felt Eleese's baby. I liked touching her cheeks and smelling her hair. She was so soft. I've never felt anything so soft before."

"Oh, who is Eleese?"

Olive shrugged once again and never took her eyes from the comforter. "She was at Tammy's house when I got there. She had a baby."

"Is she still there?"

"No. They took her away."

"Oh. I'm sorry." Tears rolled instantly down her cheeks and the thoughts that rolled through her mind threatened to buckle her in two. How did the Smiths live with themselves?

Changing the subject, Charly picked up a package with a queen size comforter and the matching sheets. Then she nodded to Olive. "Which ones do you like? I see one with horses on it over there." She pointed to a table with a cute little comforter in red and tan.

Olive's brows bunched slightly then she turned and looked at all the comforters in the store.

"I really like horses. Haylie loves horses. She said one day she was going to own a bunch of them." She walked around the room, feeling each comforter, one by one, letting her hand roam on the fabric. After twenty minutes she looked at Charly. "I want one like you have."

Those damned tears once again filled her eyes and Olive wavered in front of her as they altered her vision.

"Are you sure? I thought you liked the horses."

Olive shrugged. "I do, but I also like Eleese's baby. Her name was Shiloh."

Swallowing and pulling at the comforters under the table she found a twin sized comforter and then matching sheets and handed them to Olive. "Here you go. Let's go pay for them and take them home and admire our room."

12

S am walked out of the station, eager for some fresh air and a break from the investigation. Sometimes that was all he needed to think clearly about things. His mind today kept floating back to Charly and he was now sorry he'd asked her out. Well, not sorry really, just that he didn't want her to feel obligated with all she had going on.

"Hey, Sam, I've got something for you."

He turned to see Rory standing in the door of the station.

"Yeah?" Sam strode back up the sidewalk.

"I found three possible houses that could be N4309 and green. There are a few variations and just to be thorough, I found all houses that had those numbers, in any order. There's nothing here in Lynyrd Station but there are two possibilities in Saginaw Village and one in Paxton.

Sam took the sheet of paper Rory offered and read the list of addresses, separated by town. "Looks like an afternoon road trip is in order."

Rory chuckled. "I'd offer to help, but I'm on my way out to a B&E."

"No worries. Take care of your B&E, I've got this."

Sam turned and headed toward his vehicle, finally feeling the weight lift from his shoulders with each step. With luck on his side, he'd find the house and Tammy and Junior Smith. He paged quickly through the pages and took a deep breath.

On his way out of town, he stopped at a local coffee shop and got an iced coffee to go and a granola bar to keep him from stopping somewhere less healthy. Merging into the right lane to get on the highway to Saginaw Village, he remembered something in the evidence room that had his mind tied in knots. He pulled over to the side of the road and turned on his flashers. Reaching forward to pull his phone from its holder on the dashboard, he tapped to open his pictures and scrolled through them. There it was, 39.7941. Numbers scrawled in ink on the inside of the floor joists after they'd pulled up the loose floorboards. It was hard to read and at the time he thought maybe they were measurements. Carpenters often wrote their measurements on the side of boards they were working on. But not like that. Not that many, that wouldn't signify inches and feet. He then looked at the list of addresses Rory had given him. There in small print under the addresses were the coordinates. Sam looked closely at the coordinates and compared them to the numbers in his pictures. They were similar but not the same.

He tapped his phone for the station and called Rory.

"Richards."

"Hey, remember that photo from the crime scene and the numbers written on the inside of the floor joist?"

"Yeah, some carpenter with bad penmanship scribbled something on the inside."

"I'm wondering if those are coordinates to something."

"Okay. We'd need the other coordinate to find where that is, and what do you think would be there?"

Sam stared out the windshield. "I don't have an answer bud. I'm on my way out to look at the houses you found with the same numbers in the address. Now what if those coordinates are the other house?"

"Why would they only write the coordinates and not the address?"

"I don't know. To protect themselves in case one house was found out?"

He heard Rory's chair squeak and knew he'd just leaned back and was thinking. "That could be. Here's something else. We didn't even know about the guns until we were in the house. RAPTOR was watching the house for kids, they suspected that. What if there are other illegal activities this family was involved in?"

"It's not that farfetched."

"It isn't. The captain dropped a report on your desk right after you left. Says Harry Smith has a brother, Howie Smith. Howie is married to Tammy Smith. The Smith

brothers are the sons of William Smith as in W. Smith
Cigar and Tobacco. Remember him? We haven't heard
much about him lately, but he's been in trouble with the
law for eons."

"Well, I'll be damned. His file is a mile thick."

"Right, so no telling what his two bad seeds are up to. So
far, clearly child trafficking and gunrunning."

"It shouldn't surprise me and yet it always does. When's
the funeral for Harry?"

"Tomorrow at two o'clock."

"I guess I'm going to a funeral tomorrow."

"Right." Rory's chair squeaked again. "Where are you
going now?"

"I'm heading back to Harry Smith's house right now. We
haven't released it to the family yet and I want to see if I
can find another coordinate in that house. Now that I have
a better idea of what I'm looking for, I might get lucky and
find more."

"Okay. Call if you need anything."

Making a U-turn in the road, Sam headed back to the
house where Harry Smith was killed. The adrenaline he
got when he was onto something began coursing through
his body. It could have been the coffee he'd been drinking
too. He smiled to himself; he was going to crack this case
and help Charly find Haylie Tomms for Olive. If all he
ever got was the satisfaction of helping Charly and those
girls, he'd learn to live with it.

As he turned onto the street where the house was, he saw the yellow crime scene tape blowing in the slight breeze up ahead. People walking by stopped and stared at the house, no doubt asking themselves if they ever heard or saw something they should have been alarmed about and called police. It didn't take long for word to spread in a small town and it didn't take long for the embellishments to begin either.

As he pulled his car to the curb, he took a deep breath and let it out slowly before opening his door and getting out. He walked deliberately to the back door, where he'd entered yesterday, just so those on the sidewalk wouldn't have anything to see inside when he opened the door.

The smell inside the house was cloying. The windows and doors were closed up, the smell of death still hung in the air along with the blood and gunpowder. Things looked different because many things had been moved or taken into custody when police left yesterday. He walked into the living room and saw the boards still pulled off their resting places and off to the side. Navigating the three holes in the floor, he kneeled down and shined his flashlight inside, looking for more numbers or coordinates or anything that would help him piece this puzzle together.

13

Charly finished dressing after her shower and quietly opened the door to the bedroom in case Olive was still sleeping. Stepping into the bedroom, she glanced over and saw Olive's face peaceful in sleep and Charly smiled. It had been a hard day for Olive yesterday, today would be as well. Olive needed to have a visit to the doctor to make sure she was okay. Olive shared yesterday that she'd never been to a dentist; that would be next.

Charly sat on the edge of her bed and reached over for her prosthetic. It attached to her via an implant at the end of what was left of her arm, which was just below her left elbow. She connected the prosthetic onto the metal implant and clicked it into place.

"Does it hurt?"

She turned to see Olive sitting up in her bed watching.

"No. Not anymore. Just some phantom pain once in a while."

"What's phantom pain?"

Charly turned her body so she faced Olive. "It means, sometimes my mind still thinks my left arm is here. And sometimes it feels like my fingers hurt, like if someone squeezed your wrist so hard it cut off circulation to your fingers and they hurt. But I have no way to make it better because I don't really have fingers there anymore."

Olive scooted off her bed and came to sit on Charly's bed, facing her. She reached out and touched the prosthetic hand, running her small fingers down each of the false fingers on Charly's left hand. "Your hand was skin colored yesterday, today it's black."

Charly reached into the drawer of her nightstand and pulled out a skin-toned glove-like covering. "I put this over the top of it so it looks more human. It makes people feel more comfortable."

Olive shrugged. "What about you? Are you comfortable?"

"I can't feel it either way so it makes me feel more normal when people aren't constantly staring at me."

Charly began rolling the glove over her hand, ensuring each finger was positioned correctly before moving up her arm. Once she'd covered the entire prosthetic, the glove pulled up over her arm to cover the metal implant, or stump as she called it. From a distance it was hard to tell. It only became more noticeable when she moved it because it was slower. She'd become so adept with her right hand that it usually took a while for anyone to notice.

Olive then once again brushed her hand up and down the arm and Charly turned her hand palm up for Olive to lay her hand inside.

"I'm sorry." Olive whispered.

"You have nothing to be sorry about. Nothing at all. I'm so much better off than many of my military brothers and sisters. I have a fantastic job. I live in a nice place. I eat well, have friends, and now I have you. There is nothing to be sorry for."

Olive nodded then looked up into her eyes. "Okay."

Charly took a deep breath and changed the subject. "So, today you have a doctor's appointment with Isi. That's Dr. Isabella Masters and her husband Josh, who works for GHOST next door. She's a fantastic doctor and she'll be checking you over to make sure you're healthy. I won't lie, she'll likely need to take a blood sample to run some tests. They'll check for vitamin levels and all sorts of medical tests to see if you need anything in particular in your diet. Usually, doctors are worried about your iron levels and things like that. But that's easily treated with a vitamin or more milk in your diet."

"She's going to check to see if I'm a virgin too, isn't she?"

Charly's eyes widened. "How do you know about such things?"

"Tammy complained all the time about it. She said we couldn't let any boys touch us because we were worth more money if we were virgins and they could check and tell."

Charly's throat clogged and she swallowed a few times to moisten it. "She'll likely check you for that but not because of money. Only because girls have special needs that need to be tended to as we get older. Such as one day soon, you'll begin getting your period. Isi will need to make sure everything is healthy in your body."

Olive nodded. "I know. That's when Tammy said they'd sell us. When we started to bleed."

Charly wrinkled her nose at the crassness of Tammy and likely scaring these girls. "Is there anything you want to ask me about that?"

Olive's eyes were earnest when she looked into Charly's. "Does it hurt to bleed?"

Charly shrugged and cocked her head to the left. "Well, all I can tell you is that everyone is different. I used to get pretty bad cramps just before my period but over the years that has subsided some. Other girls don't get cramps as bad. There's no way to know how they'll affect you, but there are medicines we can take to make it a bit easier to get through. So, if that happens, you just need to let me or someone else know. Deal?"

"Deal." Olive stood then and bent to pull the covers up on her bed.

Charly smiled at her. "Did you sleep good last night?"

"I did. My sheets are really soft and warm."

"Mine too." Charly stood and pulled her sheets and comforter up and quickly made her bed.

She turned to Olive. "Get dressed and we'll go down to breakfast."

"Okay." Olive walked to the dresser and opened the drawer where her clothes were stored and pulled out one of the outfits from Callie and a new pair of underwear Charly had purchased for her yesterday. She then went into the bathroom and closed the door.

Charly walked out to the living room and took a moment to call Hadleigh. It had been weighing on her mind all day yesterday. She'd promised Olive she wouldn't lie to her and that meant she had to get real about what the realities of their situation were. Then, she needed to call Shelby to see if she could watch Olive after her doctor's appointment because Charly had a job to do and that was to find Haylie.

Tapping Hadleigh's picture, she sat on the sofa and listened to the phone ring.

"Good morning, Charly, how are you and Olive?"

"We're good. How are you and Van?"

Hadleigh laughed, "We're good. Really good."

"Glad to hear it." She took a deep breath. "Hadleigh, I need to know your thoughts on my situation with Olive. I don't want to lie to her or give her false hope. I also don't want to get my own hopes up. What do you think my chances are of being able to keep Olive?"

She heard Hadleigh take a deep breath and let it out. "I honestly think your chances are slim, Charly. And please know that doesn't mean anything about you as a person. But the system is stringent on placements for adoption.

You're single. You have a dangerous job and one that takes you away sometimes for days. You live in a close community, but for a child like Olive, that could be seen as dangerous in that there are men there all the time who aren't related to her."

Charly let the stupid tears fall from her eyes and allowed herself a minute to catch the wind that had just been punched out of her.

"Oh honey, I'm so sorry." Hadleigh continued. "I know you have special feelings for Olive and I promise you, we'll do everything we can to make sure she goes to the very best home. Not a foster home but a proven home with people who want children."

"Yeah." Charly's voice cracked. "Yeah."

She heard the bathroom door open and sniffed. "I've got to run, Hadleigh, we're going down for breakfast."

She swiped at her face and eyes and took a deep breath before Olive walked into the room.

14

Sam snapped photos of the numbers he found. Two separate sets of numbers were written inside one of the holes in the floor separated by a few inches. He looked around the living room area and saw another section of flooring that had been picked up closer to the stairs to the second level; he found another set of numbers inside and snapped the picture.

Deciding to check out the upstairs, he slowly made his way up the dark enclosed stairwell. The walls needed paint and a thorough cleaning. The steps and floor at the top were dirty and looked as though they hadn't been cleaned in years. The faint musty odor caused his nose to wrinkle and his stomach twisted at the thought of all the kids that had to endure this place. The first room at the top of the steps and to the left was clearly where Harry Smith or some other adult slept. The bed was unmade and things were toppled over, likely from their search, but it seemed like an adult room. The comforter on the bed, though bunched up, was a dark blue with red stripes running along one half of it. Few personal items were kept there, no pictures on the wall, nothing on the dresser that would tell a person lived there. As if it were a second home or a temporary setup.

Sam walked to the closet, the door open and hanging from the top hinge only. The bottom had broken off, causing it to tilt toward him. The smattering of clothing in the closet confirmed a short stay.

Sam walked from the first room to the room across the hall, which was just as depressing. An old blanket lay on top of dirty sheets and a rumpled pillow lay at the head of the bed. No dresser was in the room, no pictures, not even a chair, just this sad bed. A closet door across the room was closed and Sam walked to open it only to find it stuck. Pulling with both hands, he got it open although nothing was inside. Then he remembered Olive saying Harry kept guns in the room where he slept, so Sam went back across the hall and did a better search. None of the floorboards were pulled up in the room. Sam carefully walked across the whole floor, listening for a squeaking or loose board. When that turned up nothing, he walked to the dresser and opened each drawer. The top drawer held a couple pairs of underwear and socks, but nothing else.

He pulled open the second drawer, which spanned the dresser across the front, unlike the side-by-side top drawers, and found nothing but some old magazines and newspapers. He pulled the magazines out to see two of them were travel magazines from two years ago. One was a gun catalogue. The newspapers were old and folded carefully as if saving them. His brows furrowed and he wondered why the police didn't take these to look them over. He pulled them out and stacked them neatly on the dresser; there were four of them. He'd bring them to the station, catalogue, and look them over himself.

Closing that drawer, he pulled open the third drawer which also spanned the front of the dresser, and found it had a couple of sweaters folded haphazardly and nothing else.

He pulled open the bottom drawer, and noticed that it was much lighter than the drawer above it. His brows drew close again and he kneeled down to take a closer look. A couple of kids toys were laying in the bottom, a wooden carving of a horse, and a child's blanket in yellows and greens, faded at this point. Sam picked up the blanket and something rolled in the bottom of the drawer. A bullet. A single bullet.

Opening the blanket, he shook it for more and found nothing. He removed each toy from the bottom of the drawer and ran his hands along the bottom, but found nothing. He closed that drawer and opened the drawer above it and noticed once again how heavy it was compared to the others.

He ran his hands along the bottom of the drawer and noticed movement in the right back corner of the drawer bottom. As he pushed, it moved again. Looking closer at that corner of the dresser he saw scrapes and cuts in the back of the drawer and his heart started racing. Sam pulled the small knife from his pocket and opened it. Carefully sliding the blade along the back corner, he added a bit of pressure and lifted up. The bottom of the drawer lifted and he grabbed the corner with his other hand and pulled it up. There lay neatly lined boxes of ammo, largely 44 Magnum, 45 Cap, and a few boxes of rifle-caliber bullets.

He pulled his phone from his pocket and tapped the station's number.

"Hey Sam, it's Ty, what's up?"

"Ty, I'm at the Smith house and found more evidence that needs to be brought in and catalogued. Can you send someone over?"

"You bet. I actually just got back to the station so I'll run over there now."

"Thanks, Ty."

Even that quantity of bullets wasn't enough for all the guns they found, so Sam left the drawers as they were and went in search of more. He walked down the hall and to the last bedroom. It looked much the same as the one across the hall from the main room. Only a bed and no other furniture to speak of.

Olive had said Harry kept guns in his room; there had to be another hiding spot. Sam walked back to the main bedroom and on a whim, he picked up the mattress and voilà, there was a stash.

The fabric covering the box spring had been cut open and inside, there neatly lay guns and ammo. The entire length and width of the bed was covered in guns and ammo.

A squeak from downstairs had him turning to the door. The footsteps were slow and deliberate walking across the floor but he couldn't see who was there. Listening he could tell it was someone surveying the living room and he slowly pulled his gun from its holster. Ty wouldn't be here yet.

Moving to the door frame slowly so he didn't make noise, he peered around the door and waited, his gun pointed up but ready.

The soft footsteps came closer to the stairs but from his spot he couldn't see who was there. He didn't trust the Smiths not to come in even though it was still a crime scene and he took a deep breath, not knowing what he'd find.

The first step squeaked slightly and he knew someone was coming up; he waited, focusing on his breathing, and listened. Another step then another until he heard the final footfalls on the top of the stairs and coming toward him. He squared his shoulders and tried peering around the door frame.

"What are you doing here?"

15

Charly jumped. "For fuck's sake Sam, you scared the shit out of me."

"You scared me. What are you doing here?"

"I suspect the same thing you are. I'm looking for clues or information that might lead me to Haylie."

Sam looked at her closely. As in he stared.

"Have you been crying?"

She swallowed past the large lump in her throat. Her emotions were still pretty fragile from this morning and she didn't want to cry. Again.

"A little."

Sam stepped closer to her, slid his gun in its holster and as gentle as a feather, his big ol' hands cupped her face. His thumbs brushed her cheeks and his eyes, oh those unusual eyes, one blue, one green, stared into hers. And then her tears fell. His tenderness made her cry again.

He pulled her to his body and wrapped his arms around her and she felt safe and secure; she couldn't remember the last time she'd felt like that. So she sobbed into his chest. Her head only reached his mid chest, but it was firm and warm against her cheek. His hands soothed her back and held her while she cried. She could have stayed there for hours, but someone came into the house downstairs.

"Sam?"

Sam cleared his throat. "Upstairs, Ty."

She stepped back and swiped her face; Sam reached into his front pocket and pulled out a handkerchief and handed it to her.

"It's clean."

She giggled slightly but quickly dabbed at her eyes and wiped her nose.

"I didn't think men carried these anymore."

"My mom insisted and it's amazing how you get used to having something at your disposal, then when you don't, you miss it."

"Wow." She couldn't say anything else, there weren't words right now. And, as crazy as it sounded, how was it she never thought of Sam having a mom? Or a dad. Then she wondered if he had siblings and nieces and nephews. For that matter, did he have his own kids? She didn't even know that. So many things to find out about this man.

Charly stepped back and took in a deep cleansing breath. Ty Anderson jogged up the stairs and entered the room in the blink of an eye. She knew him from the police department, though not that well.

"Hi Sam. Oh, hi Charly. What brings you here?"

Sam took over the conversation so she didn't have to say anything just yet.

"Ty, here's what I found."

He lifted the mattress and Ty whistled. Then Sam walked to the dresser and Charly turned to see what he was doing.

"And here's a bunch of ammo. But not enough for all the guns we found so I suspect there's more in this house. Or the other house as Olive has mentioned."

"Okay. Wow, that's huge. I'm going to call in support for this."

"Sounds good. I'm going to keep looking. Ty, Charly's here to do her own investigation. She's working to find Haylie Tomms and the little sister, Olive, has said that she was with Haylie at another house. So, we're hoping to find some evidence that will help us find that other house."

"Sounds good."

Sam nodded at her and she turned and left the room. He followed her out and into the hallway. "There's nothing in the other two rooms other than a bed. If he kept kids in those rooms, it seems logical he wouldn't keep guns for fear they'd find them and use one on him. Which, it seems, happened anyway."

She took a deep breath and let it out. "Yeah. Did you find anything so far?"

"Yeah, let me show you."

He held his hand out toward the stairs and she turned and descended them. She could feel his presence behind her the whole way. It felt good. Really good.

At the bottom of the steps, he took her hand in his. Her left hand, which made her pause, only to have him tug her along. They walked around the two holes in the floor and into the dining room. There he stopped and faced her, his hands on her shoulders.

"What's going on with you?"

She squared her shoulders and cleared her throat.

"Hadleigh told me I likely won't be able to keep Olive. Or Haylie when we find her. I'm single, have a dangerous job, no home, all of the stuff that won't make me a good mom."

"That's not what that means, Charly."

"Well, it may as well. It means I'm not good enough for the state to see me as a fit parent."

"The state doesn't even know who you are. They don't know who anyone is. For fuck's sake, they didn't even follow up with Olive after you got her back a couple years ago. The state shouldn't be judging anyone on parenting or anything else."

She inhaled deeply and smiled. "I agree with you. But until we can get the whole system changed, it doesn't look good for me. But I promised her I'd fight tooth and nail to make sure she goes to a good home and I will for certain do that."

"I have no doubt you will. Speaking of, where is she now?"

She looked up at Sam and smiled. She still carried his hanky in her right hand, so she tucked it in her front pocket. She'd wash it and give it back to him.

"Skye Winters came over this morning to take Callie and Anders out to her house. It's her day to teach, and she and Lincoln just bought two horses so the kids were crazy to see them. Bridget was taking Wyatt out and Olive was invited and so danged excited to see the horses. Then Skye told her she could likely ride one and she..." Charly had to pause a minute. "Sam, her face. You should have seen it. She looked excited. Hopeful. She's had so little good in her life and she looked like a normal happy kid."

Sam chuckled and she liked the way his face looked when he smiled. "She is a normal kid. She's just had some rough experiences. But, she has you as a fairy godmother looking over her, so she's going to be just fine because you're fierce."

Charly laughed and before she could think, Sam had scooped her up off the floor, wrapped his arms around her and kissed her. It was beautiful. Slow. Soft. Consuming. His lips melded to hers and it felt...so...right.

16

———

Sam continued to mold his lips to Charly's and enjoy the way her body felt against his. Her small frame fit to him so perfectly he didn't want to let go. Then she wrapped her legs around his hips and his body shot into overdrive. Not exactly a romantic place to have a first kiss, but she looked so vulnerable and he'd been thinking about her for months now. He didn't know when they'd be able to have a date, or time alone together. So he took the chance, and he'd be reliving the feel of her for a long time. Her scent imprinted on his brain. She smelled like a combination of citrus and sandalwood and cinnamon and all things good and clean and pure. Her arms wrapped around his neck. Her right arm was soft and warm, her left arm was firm and cooler. When she moved her left hand the faint hum of a motor inside her arm buzzed by his ear, and if it were anyone but Charly, he'd feel differently, but he liked that she was different. Unusual. But so sexy, and they had their jobs in common. She was spunky, smart, drop dead gorgeous, and right now, she was in his arms.

She pulled away slightly and looked into his eyes. Hers were so blue, like a summer sky. He felt slightly embarrassed by his two-colored eyes.

She kissed the tip of his nose and dropped her legs, prompting Sam to set her down. Which he did not want to do. But he did. Slowly. Letting her body slide down his.

Car doors slamming outside had them stepping apart and he already missed her.

"Okay, back to work. But, for the record, I really want to repeat that. Soon."

She smiled and his heart beat a bit faster. "Me too."

He nodded once and walked over to the lifted floorboards showing her the numbers written on the inside.

"I think these are GPS coordinates. As soon as I have all of them, I'll go back to the office and run some searches."

"I can have Cyber Team do it now. It'll save us some time."

Charly took pictures of the coordinates in each hole in the floor and forwarded them to Piper. "It doesn't take them long. They're good."

She smiled and he knew how proud she was to work with people so damned skilled at their jobs. He felt the same way about his coworkers.

"Okay. Then, we need to search in the kitchen. Olive said something about Harry storing guns in the kitchen, but I didn't see anything in evidence that mentioned being found in there. I believe there's still a cache somewhere."

"Okay, let's go." Charly led the way and it enabled him to watch her walk away, which was no hardship at all. Not at all.

The front door opened and he turned around to see two police officers enter. Recognizing them as newer hires, he chastised himself for not knowing their names. In his defense, he'd only met them in passing when they were introduced in a staff meeting and he was focused on a case. He pointed upstairs and they nodded and walked up without a word.

As soon as he entered the kitchen, he found Charly on all fours looking in the bottom cabinets. He took a deep breath and let it out, then turned to look on the other side of the room. She was a temptress and she didn't even know it.

"Do we need to take pictures before we move anything?"

Sam turned to see Charly sitting on the floor and facing him.

"Did you find something?"

"Yep." She pointed to the cabinet to the right of the sink. "There's a cubby up there," she pointed, "with what I think is a 9mm."

Sam walked over to where she sat and kneeled down alongside her. She scooted over for him to get his body under the cabinet, pulling his phone out for the flashlight function as he did. Looking up inside the cabinet he saw not one cubby but four of them, one in each corner of the cabinet. Guns were stuffed into each cubby.

"Nice work Charly."

"Thanks." He snapped pictures and made notes on them on his phone.

Charly's phone sounded a text and she opened it immediately.

"Piper and Caiden found information. The numbers are coordinates, just as you suspected, and lead to four different areas outside of Indianapolis."

She tapped her phone and a map populated with four pins marking the coordinates. Using two fingers she enlarged the map around each of the pins and furrowed her brow.

"None of these are houses." She frowned slightly as she studied the map. "These are all just off the highway, there aren't any buildings."

Sam studied the map with her as his mind raced to figure it out. "I wonder if there's something buried there?"

Charly looked up at him and wrinkled her nose. "As in bodies?"

Sam shrugged. "Could be more guns. Could be money. Could be something else."

"Right." She took a deep breath. "What do you have to do to get someone to go out there and dig in those areas?"

He cleared his throat. "If we're lucky the landowner will oblige us and let us dig. If not, if they're protecting something, we'd have to get a court order."

Charly shrugged. "I can have a team out there without any of that."

"What about the landowner?"

She shrugged. "What about them? Usually money talks. If they're hiding something, we'll just go in under darkness. We have access to imaging equipment. We'd image the area and see if we can tell what's there. If it is bodies, all we have to do is threaten the owner with prison for hiding corpses. You'd be amazed how quickly they cave. Unless they're guilty."

She texted Piper back and asked for information on the landowners. She then turned and began searching again. "I still need to find that other house and Haylie."

He nodded and thought how inefficient the police department was sometimes. Or maybe how constraining following the law was.

Charly exclaimed. "Here we go."

17

Charly found a false wall in a tiny broom closet at the back. She pushed on it and it moved, so she pushed harder. The top corner pushed in and she pushed further.

Sam came up alongside her. "Let me push on it, Charly."

"I hope you're not insinuating that because I'm a girl I can't do this."

He chuckled. "Babe, I'd never say that about you. You are one of the most capable women I've ever seen. But, allow me to be somewhat chivalrous and help out."

She grinned and stepped back. Besides she got to stare at him while he worked and that was the good part.

He pushed on it once, nice and hard, and it gave way. He chuckled, "Well, I guess if we'd looked, we'd have seen the latch at the bottom."

She looked at where he pointed and shrugged. "Yep."

He bent, undid the latch and pulled the panel out of the closet and they both stood and stared.

"Holy shit," she exclaimed.

"Yeah. Holy shit is right."

Sam took pictures of the shelves built into the back of the closet and the rows of notebooks standing inside. There must have been more than forty of them.

Once Sam finished with the pictures, Charly reached in and pulled out a few of the notebooks. There were a variety of them, some spiral bound, some tablets, there were three or four three-ring binders and a couple of ledger books. Could they be so lucky?

Flipping open the notebook on top, she saw dates written fairly neatly down the left side of the page. Next to each date was a dollar amount and next to the dollar amount were two sets of initials. There was a blank line in between each row of data. The notebook's dates began in 2000.

"Oh my God, that's more than twenty years. They've been doing this for more than twenty friggin' years!"

Sam looked over her shoulder and she could hear his breathing grow shallow and fast. "That doesn't say much for me and the department does it?"

"I don't think that at all. Clearly they've been very good about staying under the radar."

She turned and looked at Sam. "Which has me wondering how long they've owned this house. Do you have that information?"

"No, we can get it. And, speaking of that, I did get a couple of leads, which I was going to next, on houses in Saginaw Village and Paxton. They have similar numbers to the house numbers Olive saw."

"Why didn't you tell me that right away?"

"I was focused on the evidence and I didn't want you to go alone."

Charly turned and faced him, her hands on her hips and irritation in her eyes. At least that's what she hoped she conveyed.

"You didn't want me to go alone?" She kept her tone even, but she was feeling anything but even right now.

"It could be dangerous."

"So what? You think I haven't seen dangerous?" She lifted her left arm to prove her point and he winced.

"I know you've seen dangerous. But you don't have to see it alone."

She turned and walked to the door but Sam caught her around her waist and held her back to his front. His voice lowered and his low sultry voice in her ear while he was holding her was a turn-on, even through her irritation at him. And that made her madder still.

"Charly. I don't think you understand my past. It's just that I've seen some...I lost a partner. She went into a situation without me. I let her go, not realizing the danger. She was shot and I wasn't there. It was my responsibility to protect my partner and her responsibility to do the same. I failed her. I can't fail you. I can't, Charly."

She sucked in a deep breath and let it out, forcing herself to see his point. But, still, she had a job to do and she was going to help Haylie Tomms. Olive depended on her. She demanded it of herself. She slowly turned to face him, but stepped back so she could look up into his eyes.

"I'm sorry to hear about your partner. I am. But I'm not your partner. And I can take care of myself. And, I have eight teammates I can and will call if I see something I think is suspicious. I'm not stupid and I won't go in blind."

He stared at her for a long time and she wondered what he was thinking. She saw his eyes glisten and worried he'd cry. She didn't know how to handle that. She also wondered if he'd been in love with his partner. Why that popped into her head she didn't know. Maybe because of the emotion he was currently displaying.

She watched him swallow. He opened his mouth to say something and the words didn't follow. He cleared his throat and started again.

"Charly. Please let me go with you. I'll let you call the shots, but can we compromise on this?" He didn't break eye contact with her and then as soft as you please he said, "Please."

That did it. She caved. "Alright."

He leaned down quickly and kissed her lightly on the lips. Not like before, but still, she liked it. Then he straightened. "I'll go up and tell the officers to catalogue these notebooks too. Then we can go."

"What if there's information in them that will lead us to the house?"

He looked at the notebooks then back at her. "It's your call. Dig through the notebooks, or go check out the houses I have addresses on, and see if they look like anything we might want to investigate further."

She exhaled and thought for a moment. She didn't want to waste any time. But which was the larger waste?

"Okay. Give me the addresses and I'll see if Cyber can get satellite pictures of the houses. While they're doing that, we can go through the notebooks and see if we can find something. That, along with the information on when this house was purchased and in what name, may give us enough information to save us some time."

She stepped closer to Sam, "Now, how do you feel about that?"

"You need to promise me if there is something going on that's outside the lines of the law, you have to tell me so I can step aside."

"I will. We're not criminals, Sam."

"I know you aren't, but you do tend to step over the lines from time to time, and we look the other way because it's for the greater good. But I don't want to lose my job by getting caught up in something I shouldn't. I won't be able to move to a larger city and bigger station if I'm caught doing something untoward."

"Wait, you want to leave Lynyrd Station?"

18

Sam stared at Charly and saw so much in her expression. The first of which made his stomach twist—sadness.

"It's not like I'm dying to get out. It's just that I always wanted to lead a department of detectives. There are so many skills I have that aren't used here in Lynyrd Station. When I was in the military, I was a leader. I ran squads. Here, I'm one of two detectives and the other detective, Rory Richards, is above me. This is his hometown, so he isn't going anywhere. Which means I'll always be number two."

Charly took a deep breath and stepped back. "I don't look at you as number two."

Sam closed his eyes for a moment and sighed. "I didn't mean for this to get heavy or to turn on us. It's just I've always wanted to be in a bigger station with more to offer than Lynyrd Station."

"Why did you come here if it's too small?"

He watched her swallow and regretted his words. She'd already had a rough morning and now he was unintentionally adding to it. "Rory has been a friend of mine since our military days. When I got my divorce, I wanted a fresh start and he encouraged me to come here."

Charly looked into his eyes for a few beats of his heart then turned her head to look out the window. He saw it; a door closed between them, and he felt it too. And that feeling weighed heavy on his heart. But he didn't want to lie. Not to her.

"Okay, good to know. I think I'll just go check out those houses myself and once you have the notebooks catalogued let me know and maybe I'll have Emmy contact Captain Peters for sharing privileges. I can look through them with some of my team members and with a lot of luck, we'll find some addresses. After all, your job here is to find the other illegal activities. Mine is to find Haylie and stop these people from trafficking. Two different things."

She turned to walk out of the kitchen door.

"Charly. Wait..."

But she didn't. She kept walking and his heart felt as heavy as stone.

He watched her walk through the backyard and between the houses to the street behind. That's how she didn't see he was there. That's why she was surprised by him.

He began cataloguing the notebooks, feeling as though he needed to do something monotonous for a while, allowing his mind and his heart to wrap itself around what had just happened and figure out how to make it better.

Ty walked down the stairs and into the kitchen and whistled. "Wow, that's some impressive detective work, Sam."

He should have said it was all Charly, but he only nodded. "I'll catalogue these and get them back to the station so we can start going through them."

"Sounds good. I'm on my way out to the car to get more boxes and we have two more officers coming over to help with the collection."

"Sounds good. Thanks."

Sam pulled out his notebook and started with book one, snapping a photo of it, writing it out on his notebook, along with anything written on the cover.

His phone rang and he absently answered, "Bowers."

"Sam, we need you at the Nuthin' Fancy Bar. A fight broke out between a couple of customers." Captain Peters said.

"Isn't that something an officer should handle, Captain?"

"Normally yes. But this fight broke out between the son of Howie and Tammy Smith and a patron. I think we need you there to talk to the son, Phillip. Maybe you can get a location out of him. It's likely not going to be easy, but you have a knack for ferreting information out of people."

Wow, Captain had never complimented him on interrogation before. He felt a small amount of pride slip in but it was tempered by Charly's departure.

"I'll be right there, Captain. And, hey, thanks for the compliment."

"You know, Sam, I don't say this enough—and I should— but you do a fantastic job for this department, and over the last couple of years we've really needed you with all that's gone on here and apparently, continues to go on. But we'll get it all cleaned up."

"Thanks, Cap. I'm on my way out the door here."

Ty entered the house with evidence boxes. "Hey Ty, I've been called out to a situation. I'll need you guys to catalogue and pack up these notebooks as well."

"Will do, Sam." Ty nodded then walked up the steps.

Sam walked out the back door and couldn't help but look through the houses where Charly had left. He turned and walked to his vehicle on the street and tried focusing on the task he had coming up. Gathering information on where the other house was. That's what he needed to focus on now.

Upon approaching the bar, Sam noticed people standing around outside the front door. He took a deep breath before exiting his vehicle then muttered to himself, "Here we go."

As he approached the front of the bar, people turned and stepped aside upon seeing him. He'd always had that effect on people. Just his size alone was enough to intimidate people. That's likely why his interrogation was successful. But he sure hoped it was also because he was good at it.

He entered the bar and saw one of the department officers, Eydie Evans, on the scene.

"Hi, Eydie, tell me what's going on." He knew, but that was part of his tactic for getting the offenders to talk to him.

"Hi, Sam. These two men were fighting." She pointed to two men on opposite sides of the horseshoe shaped bar. Both had blood on their faces and swelling from taking punches. Both looked as though they'd gotten as much as they'd given. But one looked like he'd gotten a bit more than the other. Sam focused on him first.

He stepped in front of the man and blocked his view from the other one. "I'm Detective Sam Bowers. What's your name?"

"Richie Reynolds."

"Nice to meet you, Richie. Now, can you tell me what happened here?"

"That jackass over there came into the bar and sat right next to me. I told him to move. I actually told him to leave. I don't like him or his no-good family. They're all bad. They broke into my house a couple of years ago and stole a couple of my guns. His dad was there, too. This jerk..." He leaned around Sam and pointed. "Was there and high as a fucking kite. Pointed his gun at my wife and called her a whore."

"Did you call the police?"

His voice lowered. "No. I was afraid I'd get in trouble for not having the guns secured better."

"You should have called the police, Richie. If the guns were in your house and those guys broke in, that's breaking and entering. If they had guns and robbed from you, that's armed robbery. We could have put them away."

"They said they have a judge in their back pocket and it'd do no good."

Sam looked him in the eyes. His left eye was beginning to turn purple now but he never looked away. "Did he say which judge?"

"No, but everyone knows it's Kissinger."

"Who's everyone? I've never heard that."

Richie shrugged and Sam waited for him to say more, but he didn't.

"Okay. We can look into that a bit later. So, you told him to get out and what happened next?"

"Fucker sucker-punched me in the side of the face. Just hauled off and punched me." He pointed to the side of his face where the skin was beginning to turn purple.

"Okay. Then what happened?"

"I straightened myself up and punched that fucker back. Got him square in the nose."

Sam nodded. "Then what?"

"We started fighting it out until some of these guys broke it up."

"Okay. I need you to stay here while I talk to Phillip."

19

Charly drove to Saginaw Village. Caiden had been able to pull up the information she needed on the houses and where they were. The drive would help her out. Plus, Olive begged to stay at the Winters' because they were having so much fun. Skye had them out on the horses. Then she had the kids brush the horses and put them away. Then they learned how to feed them. Now, they were inside learning how to measure ingredients and bake a cake. Skye was good for the kids. Charly didn't do any of that stuff.

She entered the town of Saginaw Village and followed the directions on her GPS to the first house. It had the same numbers in the same sequence as the one Olive had said she was in, N4309. Her GPS led her out the other side of town and to a county road. She watched as she drove along, trying to see anything that might look out of place, not knowing what she was looking for.

As the driveways began to stretch farther apart, she noticed the address signs began with N39. She was getting closer. A mile down the road and the addresses began with N42. She slowed her SUV and rolled her window down, laying her left arm on the window ledge to look like a casual passerby. Then she saw it.

She slowed even further, looking up the long driveway as she drove by. The house wasn't green but a lighter blue and could use a coat of paint. No cars were in the drive-way, no signs that anyone lived there, actually. There was a detached garage to the rear of the yard. The grass was mowed but the edges weren't trimmed. A small front porch held only one lone chair that had newspapers piled up on it. The mailbox had no name on it.

She looked for a place to park where she could walk in undetected from the back. The properties on either side of the house were similar in architecture but both were neater and she wondered if anyone would talk to her if she asked questions.

She drove up the drive of the neighbor to the east and parked about halfway up. Getting out of her SUV, she walked to the front door and noticed a pretty grouping of flowers in a pot on the little porch and a "Welcome" sign on the door. She knocked and looked over at the house in question to see if she could see anyone looking out the windows, but no one was visible.

The door opened and an older man opened the door.

"Hi there, can I help you?"

"Hi, my name is Charly and I have a delivery to make to your neighbor, Tammy Smith, but no one is answering. I was wondering if you knew anything about her like when she's usually home."

The older man looked over at the house and shook his head. "I'm sorry. I don't know anything about them. They stay to themselves. Won't even wave if I see them outside."

"Thank you. Have they lived there long?"

"Yeah, I guess around six or seven years or so."

Charly smiled. "Thank you. I'll try again later."

"Can't you leave it on the porch?"

"Oh, no, I have to get a signature for it."

The old man nodded. "Good luck to you."

Charly turned and walked to her car. She saw a path worn into the field between the two houses and turned to the old man.

"Where does that path lead?"

The old man stepped out on the porch further and looked at the path. "Oh, I have an old shed out back and I used to bring my tractor back there. Back in the days when I still farmed." He pointed across the main road. "My son runs the farm now, and I'm just his consultant." He chuckled. "He built an addition on to the machine shed a couple of years ago so we don't go back there anymore."

Charly nodded. "Thank you."

She got into her car and decided to come back later tonight and walk down that path to see if she could see anything inside the house after dark. She had a sneaking suspicion that this was the house that Olive described, but since she had a bit of time, she'd check out the other house in Saginaw Village and the one in Paxton, just to be sure.

As she drove past the house once again, she kept her eyes sharp hoping to see something, but it was buttoned up tight. She took a deep breath and called Skye.

"Hi Charly, what's up?"

"I'm checking in on Olive. How are things going?"

"Great. We're just getting ready to put the cake in the oven, then we're going to work on our math just a bit more."

"That sounds great. I have to work late tonight, will you be able to keep Olive for a while, or should I see if Shelby can watch her?"

"Oh, no, we can keep her. We're having fun."

"Thank you, Skye, I appreciate it."

Skye chuckled. "It's all good. Just let me know when you're ready to have her back."

"Will do. Tell her I called."

"I will."

Charly hung up and called in to headquarters to report her findings.

"Caiden Marx."

"Hey Caiden. Did you give the coordinates to Emmy?"

"I did and she sent Falcon and Creed out to do some investigation. They'll talk to the landowners too if they're around and get us access to whatever is there."

"Fantastic. I'll be out for a while. After dark I'm sneaking up to the house in Saginaw Village. I'll have my phone and I have a comm unit, so who's on tonight in case I run into issues?"

"Deacon's on tonight. I'll let him know what's going on. Do you need back up on the scene?"

"No, I'm just going to look into windows and snoop a bit."

"Sounds good. Be careful."

20

Sam walked around the horseshoe shaped bar to where Phillip stood with a cocky casual-looking stance. He was anything but casual. His fists were balled but he leaned back against the wall as if he didn't care. His jaw was set, a trickle of blood drew a red line down his face from temple to cheek and his nose had dried blood under it where he'd gotten a good shot in the snoot.

"I'm Detective Sam Bowers. What's your name please?"

"You know who I am."

"I'd like you to say it."

Sam looked down on him. The scrawny man was stick-thin with sunken cheeks, yellowed teeth, and though he wore a whitish tank top under a sloppy fitting open shirt, his ribs showed through the tank top. Nutrition was not his game.

"Phillip Smith." He spat out.

Sam stood to his full height and took a deep breath. This guy was going to be a pain in the ass and was the guy he needed to talk.

"So, would you like to tell me your side of this story?"

"Nothing much to tell. I come in and sit down and that bastard over there told me to get the fuck out. All I did was sit down. He told me I was no good and neither was my family."

"Then what happened?"

"I coldcocked that fucker. Who is he to tell me my family is bad news? He got a teenage daughter that got herself knocked up. She's whoring around town and he's jaw-jackin about my family?"

"Okay. So you hit him first then what happened?"

"He hopped off his barstool and punched me behind my ear. That's a sucker punch right there. Equivalent to shooting someone in the back's what that is."

"Well, not quite the same. But I get your meaning."

"Damn straight it's the same thing."

Sam moved to the left a bit to divert Phillip's attention from trying to look over at Richie. "Anything else you want to add?"

"Not really."

Sam pulled his notebook out of his back pocket. He wrote down Phillip's name. "What's your address, Phillip?"

"Why do you need that?"

"I have to fill out a report and need to have all of the information for it. Don't be a wise guy and try to avoid it. I'll get it anyway but I'll have to do a lot of snooping to get it and then I'm going to be pissed."

"Fine. 2218 Jackson Street."

"How long have you lived there?"

"A few years. What difference does that make?"

"No difference. I just thought you lived over on Jefferson Street."

"Naw, that's my uncle's house. He got killed there earlier this week by some kid."

Sam nodded his head as if just remembering. "Oh, that's right. I'm sorry for your loss."

"You're kidding right? You didn't know that?"

"It's not my case."

"Right."

"Hey, are you related to William Smith? As in W. Smith Cigar and Tobacco Co.?"

"Yeah. My grandpa."

"No kidding? My uncle loved going in there back in the day. He's gone now though. Is that place still open?"

"Yeah. My old man runs it now."

"Okay. Wow, I haven't thought about that place in years. I'll have to stop by one day." Sam thought conversation was best.

Phillip shrugged and Sam continued writing notes in his notebook.

"Do you work in the store?"

"No."

"Where do you work?"

"What difference does that make?"

"Report is all." Sam tapped his pen on his notebook.

"Ain't none of your business."

Sam shrugged. "Suit yourself. I'll just dig around in your personal life. Talk to people. Ask a ton of questions, but I'll find out."

"Jeeeezus you are a pain in the ass. I work for my parents."

"I thought you said you didn't work at the tobacco store."

"I don't. I do other things for them. Sort of grunt work kind of stuff. Deliveries, things like that."

Sam wrote it down and knew what deliveries the son of a bitch was making.

"I didn't realize W. Smith delivered. How long have you been doing that?"

"We don't deliver tobacco and such. It's just sometimes they need me to take things to other places. I also mow their lawns and shit. I'm just their grunt boy."

"Sounds like a shitty job."

"It is."

"Why do you stay? You could easily find something else to do."

"One day that store will be mine and I'll run it the way I want to run it."

"Fair enough." Sam continued to take notes. "There's living quarters upstairs in the store, isn't there?"

"Sort of."

"What does that mean? Your parents don't live there?"

"Naw, they live over in Saginaw Village now."

Sam's heart began beating faster. That's where he'd go next. It was one of the towns that had an address with the same numbers Olive had mentioned.

"Okay, that's all good then. I suggest you leave the bar now. Richie was here first. And make sure you keep yourself out of trouble."

Phillip scowled and pushed himself off the wall and made a big deal about leaving. Sam walked over to Officer Evans and lowered his voice.

"Follow him. Get a description of his vehicle, plates, etc. Then follow him at a distance and see where he's headed. I'll call you when I've finished up here and get the information from you."

"You got it." Eydie turned and followed Phillip out the door and Sam returned to the opposite side of the bar where Richie still stood. His arms were crossed over his chest and he looked less angry and more in pain and tired than just a few minutes ago.

"Richie, tell me what you know about Phillip Smith. Not gossip. Not conjecture. Just the facts as you know them."

Richie looked up at him with one eye. The other was swelling closed as he stood there. Sam held up a finger to stay Richie's comments and turned to the bartender.

"Call an ambulance for Richie."

He then turned back to Richie and waited. Richie took a deep breath and appeared to give his answer some thought before responding.

"He did break into my house. It was three years ago. I didn't call police because I was worried he'd come back. He's bad news. And, he's been seen lurking around by the school in the afternoons when the kids leave. I didn't want him accosting my kids. He's unpredictable and I just wanted him to forget about me and my family. But I told him, if he ever came close to my house again, I'd kill him. And I will. I'll protect my family at all costs. I won't go gunning for him, but I will protect what's mine."

Sam watched Richie's expressions, though the swelling made them appear lopsided and ghoulish. He was dead-ass serious.

"Do you know anything about his parents?"

"Hell, doesn't everyone? They run drugs or guns or something out of that old beaten-up cigar store. It looks closed from the outside on the street. I don't know anyone who goes there anymore. They moved out of town about six years ago. Moved to Saginaw Village I heard."

"What about Paxton? Hear anything about a place there?"

"I've only heard rumors."

21

Dusk had set and Charly parked her car on the edge of the road, four properties down from the Smith house. Her phone vibrated and she picked it up before exiting her vehicle.

"Charly."

"Hey Charly, it's Deacon. I just pieced a couple of the houses together. So, the one at N4309 County Road G in Saginaw Village and the one on Jackson Street where Harry Smith was killed are owned by SmithCo LLC. When I did a records search for SmithCo LLC I found that they own two more houses. Another on the county line between Lynyrd Station and Saginaw. And one in Paxton, but not the one you looked at today. That one is at W8932 County Road A in Paxton. I'll text you the addresses."

"Thanks, Deac. So, I'm getting ready to walk down the path and to the back of the house in Saginaw. Keep your comm unit on please."

"Okay, give me two minutes to get it on then I'll buzz you."

"Thanks. Out."

Charly pulled the infrared flashlight she had packed out of her go bag and checked that it worked. She checked her gun, just in case she ran into something or someone out there who meant her harm. It was loaded and ready, she then tucked it into the holster on her right hip. Her comm unit was secured in her ear, and she took a deep breath. As soon as Deacon buzzed her, letting her know without words he was listening, she'd get out of her car.

A light buzz vibrated in her ear.

Charly took a deep breath and opened her car door. The sun was now set, but the sky still had a faint orangish glow illuminating it. It gave her just enough light that she could see the road and the white reflective strips painted on the edges.

She followed that until she arrived at the area where the path began. The tall grasses grew up in the ditch around the path's beginning and partially hid it, but she'd been staring at it for the past forty minutes or so and had it imprinted on her brain.

Charly stepped off the road and onto the path, avoiding rustling through the tall grasses so she didn't make noise. She could see both houses from that vantage point, the neighbor she spoke to today and the Smith house. The neighbor's house was brightly lit in the lower level. The last vestiges of the sun's rays bounced off the upper windows, brightening it up even more.

The Smith house, in contrast, had little light shining through the windows, it looked as though blinds or curtains covered them. The only light escaping was from either side of each window and the sun's rays fell on dirty glass, obstructing its ability to reflect.

Charly continued to walk to the shed the neighbor had mentioned but kept her eyes peeled for any movement. She wished she'd asked Olive about a dog or dogs to know if she was going to encounter any animals. Luckily there'd been no sightings of wolves in the area, at least not the four-legged kind. And she chuckled to herself because it was usually the two-legged wolves who were more dangerous.

Charly reached the shed and quietly walked around it to see if there was anything of note. Pulling open the door to get in, she stepped inside and turned on her infrared flashlight, which was similar to night vision and didn't emit a bright light, to see what was inside. An abandoned looking piece of farm equipment, a disc or something similar, was to the right of the shed; the other side just held a workbench littered with a smattering of screws and nails and small pieces of metal and wood as if the workman finished his job and left the mess behind.

She stepped from the shed, confident she could hide in there if need be, and walked to the side where she could see the back of the Smith house. Her heart skittered when she saw that the back of the house at some point had received a coat of green paint. While the front looked as though it needed paint, the back had been painted within the past couple of years. She looked at the garage and where it was located and realized that's how Olive saw the green. She'd likely been brought out of the back door and only saw that as she was put into a car in the garage.

"Deac? The back of the house is green," she whispered.

"So it is the house Olive saw."

"Yes." Charly walked to the back of the garage and peered through the window. "There's a black Corolla in the garage, I'd say about a 2000 or a 2001. The plates are 839ZEZ."

"Got it and running them now."

"Okay. There's an empty space in the garage where likely a second car is usually sitting."

"Roger."

Charly stepped from behind the garage and began walking, though crouched down, to the back of the house. Reaching the back at the bottom of the small porch area that had three steps up to the back door, she stood next to the steps and looked around and listened. Hearing nothing, she slowly started ascending the steps, grateful they were cement so she didn't have to worry about squeaks.

Just as she stepped onto the second tread, lights illuminated the area along the driveway and the sound of tires crunching on the gravel stopped her in her tracks. She pushed herself against the wall as the garage door began to open and a car slowly entered the garage.

Charly waited until the car was out of sight, then scrambled down the two steps and around the backside of the steps, tucking herself into the corner against the house and the cement steps, hoping she'd not be detected.

As footsteps on the gravel began drawing closer to her, she focused on steadying her breathing and staying as small as she could. The hammering of her heart sounded loud in her own ears but her rational mind knew no one else could hear it.

The footsteps sounded on the cement as someone with boots clunked up them, the last sounding by her ear. She closed her eyes and waited, hearing a key enter the lock and the doorknob twist with a tinny clink. The door squeaked as it opened and the footsteps entered the house; the door closed.

Letting out a slow unsteady breath, she waited a few more seconds before moving, knowing if there was any activity to see, it would be now, with the entrance of another person. She stood, making sure her legs were steady, and slowly stepped away from her hiding spot.

A familiar male voice growled. "What are you doing here?"

22

S am couldn't believe his eyes. Just as he'd rounded the corner on the far side of the house, he saw Charly standing in the shadows.

"What are you doing here?" she whispered.

"I'm investigating."

"So am I."

"Charly this is dangerous. Why are you here alone?"

She could smell his aftershave, a fantastic combination of something spicy and sweet. His broad chest stretched over a three-button placket shirt of dark gray. The shirt fit him well, then tucked nicely into a pair of dark jeans. He was yummy.

"I'm just doing a check to see what we're dealing with. Deacon is in my ear."

She tapped her right ear and he saw the earpiece shine from the lights that still hadn't gone out after the car triggered them.

"Fat lot of good he'd do you in your ear if something happened to you."

"Sam, you simply don't under..."

Anger flared through him. Why was she putting herself in danger?

"Don't tell me I don't understand. I certainly do, but you come to a place like this with backup, not alone."

He saw her jaw set and her shoulders square and knew she was mad, but so was he. She looked around him to his right then his left.

"Is your backup hiding somewhere?"

"I'm not a wo..."

She hissed, "Don't you dare."

He took a deep breath. He wasn't being unreasonable. Charly was capable, certainly. But she was petite and like it or not, she had a left arm that allowed her to do so many things but it also could be a hinderance. And, she simply was no match for someone like these Smiths.

He reached forward and took her left hand in his right hand and tugged her around the side of the house. He looked up to see that all the windows were closed, then realized they could still be heard, so he pulled her to the road, crouching down as he went, then led Charly through the ditch with the tall grasses and onto the road. There he continued walking down to where he'd left his car, right behind hers. The realization that she wasn't fighting him gave him some relief.

Once they reached his car he stopped and turned to her. It was dark out, but his eyes had adjusted and the look she was giving him sent a chill down his spine.

He dropped her hand and watched as she stood stock still, glaring at him.

"Charly."

She held her right hand up between them. "Nope."

"What?"

"Nope. No. Nada. You just insulted me and the only reason I followed you back here is so you and I can have this conversation without screwing up my surveillance. Yes. Mine."

"But..."

"Let me tell you how this works Samuel Bowers." She took a deep breath and continued while he held his breath and dreaded what was to come.

"I am an operative. A fucking good one. I've trained and trained and trained. My boss wouldn't let me be out here alone if she didn't trust me to do my job with confidence and accuracy. My teammates wouldn't either. What I'm doing out here is tracking down a pedophile, perhaps more, and looking for a lost little girl, whose sister desperately wants her back."

Sam finally took a deep breath. "I know but..."

"No, no buts! Do you understand how hard I've worked to be here? Do you know the tears I've cried? Do you know the sleepless nights, the pain, the hours and hours of training I've endured to be here?"

"No, but..."

"No. There is no but. There's just me. Charly. Doing my job. And there's you."

"Doing mine." He let out a breath and Charly opened her mouth to continue to berate him, but he couldn't stop himself.

He reached forward and pulled her tightly to him, wrapped his arms around her and held her close. Then, he dipped his head down and pressed his lips tightly to hers. He expected resistance. He even halfway expected her to bite him. Even that would likely be sexy. She was without a doubt the sexiest woman he'd ever met. All of her. Every square inch of Charlesia Sampson was one thousand percent sexy woman.

Her lips softened almost instantly. Her head tilted slightly and he could taste her breath as it rushed out. She tasted amazing. When her lips then molded to his and kissed him back his body responded. The rush was so fast and furious his hands shook. He held her tighter. When she softly moaned, his tongue slipped between her lips. He heard her sigh and his cock thickened. This woman was like crack to him.

The lights of a car flashed down the road and he reluctantly pulled back. Then he stepped back slightly and looked down at her, her expression now visible with the lights of the approaching car. Her lips were puffy from his kiss and she licked her lips, which did even more unmentionable things to him.

"Charly." His voice sounded like he'd swallowed sand. "I...Let me explain."

She inhaled a deep breath and let it out slowly. Her eyes looked deeply into his, her lips parted but she said nothing.

"I care about you. I want you to always be safe. If something happened..."

His voice cracked and he felt stupid that he was suddenly emotional.

She raised her right hand and cupped the side of his face. Her thumb smoothed over his cheek, then slid down and softly swiped across his lips.

"Sam. Thank you. For caring. Thank you." She smiled softly. "I understand the dangers of my job. I accept them fully. Just as you do yours. But, these kids...they need us. They need people like us who are willing to put themselves in situations that might be dangerous. Uncomfortable. Down-right impossible sometimes to make sure they are safe. In moments like these, we are all they have."

"I lost a partner. Once. You know that. She went into a situation alone. I never, ever want to live through that again. Especially not with you."

She stepped into him and the car passed them; the light began to fade. Her arms wrapped around his waist and she squeezed him tightly.

"Then, how about we work together on this and find Haylie and put these fuckers away?"

His heart hammered in his chest as he wrapped her in his embrace and held her close. He swallowed several times to get his emotions under control. He did have to let her do her job. She wasn't one to be tamed but one to be admired and trusted. He'd seen her in action and knew how smart she was.

"How about we do that."

23

Charly smiled into Sam's chest as she held him. The thrum of his heart was strong and she kept her head against his chest for a while longer so she could hear it beat. It gave her strength to know this man, whose heart beat out a steady rhythm as she held him, his arms so strong and protective around her, wanted her to be safe, and would work with her. She'd do it anyway, protect these kids, but she'd rather do it with Sam. She'd known that for a long time. Over the past couple of months, they'd flirted, stared, and generally tip-toed around actually getting together. But since he'd first asked her out, then kissed her, it was hard to think of anything else.

She reluctantly stepped back and took a deep breath.

"So, if you mean what you said and want to help me, here's what I have. Deacon..." She closed her eyes then and mumbled, "Shit."

Sam's brows pinched together.

"Are you still listening, Deac?"

"Yes, it's very enlightening. Please go on." He snickered.

Sam's eyes opened wide and she scrunched her face in embarrassment.

"Deac, you shouldn't have...I should have shut off my comm unit."

"Why? I enjoyed listening to the smooching and tongue tango."

Her head fell back and she looked up into the dark sky. She could feel the heat in her cheeks and was thrilled that no one else could see how red she likely was.

"Don't say anything to anyone, Deac."

He merely laughed in her ear.

Sam smiled. "It's okay," he mouthed. Then, loud enough so Deacon could hear, he said, "Go ahead, Charly, tell me what you have here and I'll tell you what I've found out."

She swiped at her cheeks then cleared her throat as delicately as she could.

"Okay. So, there's a shed in the back of that house right there." She pointed.

"I did some investigating. It doesn't belong to the Smiths, but just in case they decided to use it anyway, I wanted to check it out. So, there's only a piece of farm equipment in there and some miscellaneous stuff on the work bench. But, when I came out, I saw the back of the house. It's been painted green. That's what Olive saw."

"So you're pretty sure it's the house she was in."

"Well, I was going to do a bit more snooping when you showed up. I feel pretty confident, but I'd like to get a closer look."

"Okay. What do you have in mind?"

She turned her head and looked at the house from that angle. "When whoever it was walked in the back door a few minutes ago, I noticed the door squeaked, so we can't go in that way. It looks like we'll need to climb in through a window."

"You're planning on breaking in?"

"Do you have a better idea?"

Sam reached into his back pocket and pulled out a sheet of paper. "How about we go in with a warrant?"

"You have a warrant? How did you get that?"

"Turns out the son of Howie and Tammy Smith, Phillip, was in a bar fight earlier. I was called to the scene because of the Smith connection. I found out from the man Phillip was fighting with, that Phillip broke into his house a few years ago and stole some guns. I got him to finally make a complaint and that enabled me to get a warrant. It's likely the guns are gone, or I might have them at the station from the stash we got from Harry's house. I have someone going through that now. But, nevertheless, a judge said we can search."

"Well, let's go."

"I'm waiting for backup."

"I can be your backup."

"Sorry, babe, it's got to be an officer. But you're welcome to come in with us. You snoop for signs of Haylie; I'll look for the guns and anything else that might be stolen."

"Shit. Okay. When's your backup supposed to get here?"

"I thought that was them who passed a bit ago, so I'd say, any minute now."

Sam smiled at her and she blushed. She could feel the heat hit her cheeks.

Charly looked both ways down the road and impatience cloaked her body. Haylie might be in there right now and she wanted to get her back.

Sam spoke. "Deacon, can you hear me?"

"Yes." Charly nodded then pulled her comm unit from her ear and held it between herself and Sam.

"Deacon, you may want to have one or two of your operatives go over to the old tobacco shop. Watch and make sure there's no activity once we enter the house. I'll bet they have some silent network they use to contact each other and they'll be calling or pinging each other like crazy once we go in. I don't have the manpower. Also, the house in Paxton. I suspect they move girls around frequently so no one gets comfortable."

Deacon responded. "On it. Babe." His laugh could be heard as he clicked his comm unit off.

Charly shook her head. "Asshole."

Lights shined as a car turned onto the road and both she and Sam watched as it approached. The squad pulled in behind Sam's car, lights off so as not to call too much attention to it, and Sam took a deep breath.

"Listen, Charly. As cops, we can't do anything illegal. I know RAPTOR can sometimes work outside of the lines of the law. I don't have a problem with that, but we can't. So don't do anything illegal. You're allowed in under the warrant and if you step outside of the lines, it'll toss anything we do find into unusable territory."

"I understand Sam. I'll be good." She smiled, but it looked naughty. And sexy.

Sam muttered, "I've been dreaming about it."

Charly smiled; she had too.

24

O fficer Eydie Evans stepped out of her squad car and walked toward them.

Sam motioned from Charly to Eydie, "Eydie, this is Charlesia Sampson. She's a RAPTOR operative and working with us on this case as it pertains to the kids involved."

"I've met Charly before. Nice to see you again."

"Nice seeing you, Eydie."

"Okay. So, Eydie and I will go in first. Charly, you come in behind us." He opened the trunk of his car. He looked around for a moment before asking, "Eydie, do you have another vest for Charly?"

"Yes."

Eydie popped her own trunk and went to get it. Charly glanced at him without saying anything.

"It's just in case. Safety first, babe."

She smiled and joined Eydie without a word.

Securing his vest, he checked his weapons. They knew for a fact there was no shortage of weapons in the house. If they were gunrunners, there'd be plenty, and ammo too. Hopefully Haylie would be in there as well. And with any luck, or a lot of luck, the Smiths would have no time to get to those weapons once they entered the house.

Then he and Charly could proceed with their relationship in earnest.

Happy with his weapons loaded and secured, he closed the trunk of his car and walked back to Charly and Eydie. Charly struggled slightly with the buckles on her left side, so he walked over and snapped them for her. She looked up at him and he saw it in her expression—she was going to bitch.

"Don't bother, Charly. There's nothing wrong with a little assistance here and there. Get over it."

He looked over at Eydie. "You ready?"

"Yes sir."

Eydie quietly closed the trunk on her squad car and they walked toward the house. As they walked, he had a change of mind.

"I'm rethinking this arrangement. Charly and I will go to the front door; Eydie, you go around and make sure no one decides to run out the back door when we go in the front."

"Good idea, Sam. I've called in for more back up as soon as everyone is finished processing the robbery across town."

"Thanks, Eydie."

They walked quietly toward the house. Sam and Charly waited at the edge of the driveway for Eydie to walk to the back.

Charly then spoke to Deacon. "Deac, you have ears on?"

"Yeah. Keep your head down."

"Roger that."

Sam looked at her and Charly nodded and smiled.

They could no longer see Eydie, so he set his shoulders and began walking toward the house. They stepped up on the front porch, which was littered with various items, indiscernible in the dark. Sam knocked twice on the door and waited.

"Who is it?" A faceless male voice called through the door.

"Sam Bowers, Lynyrd Station PD."

"Go away."

"Open the door."

Suddenly a loud crash sounded from the back of the house. Charly took off running around the opposite side of the house of the garage and Sam was unable to stop her before she took off. Shots were heard and Sam was torn. Should he stay in case they come out the door or run back and see what was happening? His training told him to stay and deal with this side of the house. In the end he stepped off the porch and watched from the corner of the house, which was what the inhabitants were waiting for because the door opened and a tall skinny man jumped from the house and flew over the steps and took off running.

Sam took off after him, sorry he'd put his vest on due to its weight. He watched the man courtesy of the moonlight that shined down on them. He jumped into the field between his house and the neighboring property and soon he saw Charly sprinting across the field toward the man. She was fast, and he was both impressed and worried.

She dashed faster than the man as he lost steam and Sam watched amazed as Charly dove into the air at the man and tackled him to the ground. He heard a punch, and sped up as much as he could. As soon as he reached the brawl in the field, he saw Charly throwing punches at the man on the ground and him covering his head in defense.

"Stop Charly. Stop." He called to her. Sam then leaned down and put handcuffs on the cowering man. That's when he saw it was Phillip.

"Two beatings in one day. Is that a record Phillip?"

"Fuck you."

Sam chuckled and lifted Phillip off the ground. "This time by a woman. Your friends are going to love hearing about this."

Charly stood and looked down at her left arm, checking for damage. When she looked up and saw him looking, she shrugged.

"Damned thing is expensive."

He nodded and smiled at her, but saw bruising beginning under her right eye. That pissed him off.

"Let's go Phillip. We've got some chatting to do."

Another car approached and Sam stopped and watched it pull in on the opposite side of the driveway to where all of their cars were parked on the road. He could see the lights on top of the car and felt some relief that they'd have some assistance here. Ty Anderson walked toward them and nodded. "How many are there?"

"Not sure. This jerk ran out the front door. Eydie is in the back. I heard gun shots. Go check on her."

Charly spoke up then. "You'll need an ambulance but not for Eydie. She had to shoot a man who blew out the back door pointing a gun at her. I saw it. It was justified."

Ty jogged to the back of the house calling out to Eydie as he neared.

"Ty Anderson reporting."

He ducked around the back of the house and Sam tugged Phillip along as Charly walked on the other side of Phillip. She was not a scared weak woman. His heart swelled a little larger with pride for her. He was already falling in love with her. He could feel it in his heart. In his head. Everywhere. He admired the shit out of her, but, he was falling for her.

At the back of the house he saw an older man, similar in build to Phillip laying on the ground, his breathing labored. Eydie had his hands cuffed, then rolled him to his left side to keep him as comfortable as possible.

"You shot my old man you fucking bitch cop."

Sam shoved Phillip to the ground. "Shut up, Phillip. You and your family are pieces of shit. You don't want to get shot, don't point a gun at a police officer."

"It's fucking police brutality."

"Whatever." Sam spat.

Ty Anderson was on his phone calling for an ambulance and any available officers to help out with the scene.

Sam looked at Eydie and said, "I'm going to check out the rest of the house."

She nodded and Ty responded, "I'll go in with you. You have this covered Eydie?"

"Yeah. This one isn't going anywhere." She pointed to the older man, who must be Howie Smith. She then looked at Phillip, "And this one can't go anywhere with his ankles in cuffs too."

With that she held her hand out for Sam's cuffs, which he handed over and she knelt to cuff him down.

Sam nodded to Ty then looked over at Charly, to see she was walking toward the house. His brows lifted and she replied, "I'm going in too."

He entered first, gun out, carefully checking the area before nodding and Ty and Charly entered behind him. Charly also had her gun out, she understood the formation without coaching, and he smiled.

After clearing the kitchen, he entered the next room, which looked like it should be a dining room, but was instead littered with boxes and haphazardly stacked old furniture. The place reeked of cigarette smoke, which was no surprise since they owned a tobacco store. The dining room or junk room was cleared and he moved to the living room. Old filled ashtrays, ratty furniture, a wadded-up blanket in the corner of the sofa, and a television, which was still turned on were all that was in the room.

After that room was cleared, they started moving up the steps, one at a time. At the top of the steps, were three rooms. The house was almost identical to the house in Lynyrd Station where Harry Smith was killed. The first room held a bedroom set, with bed, dresser, and tall boy. The closet doors were open and the clothes hanging inside were neatly arranged. Quite a difference from the downstairs.

They cleared the room and went across the hall to the next room. That room looked like the second room at the Harry Smith house. A small bed in the room and nothing else. On the bed was a blanket with horses on it, a pillow with a white pillowcase, and a magazine.

The back bedroom was the same as the second bedroom.

The ambulance arrived and Sam went downstairs to supervise the loading of Howie Smith. Then another police officer came and he asked that Phillip Smith be taken to the station for questioning. He whispered to the officer, "Just put him in the holding cell and let him sit till morning. I want him ready to cooperate."

"Will do Sam."

He then pulled his phone from his back pocket and called his captain.

"What's going on over there Sam?"

"We've got a shit show here Captain. Howie Smith shot, Phillip Smith is on his way to the station to sit for a while, no one else is in the house and now we need to start searching for guns and ammo."

"Find what you need to go back in. Secure the house for the night and tomorrow when we have more resources, we'll go back to catalogue and collect."

"Thanks Captain."

"Sure. No sign of Haylie Tomms?"

"No." Sam felt bad about that because he knew Charly wanted to find her so badly. They all did, but it had become personal to Charly.

25

She was bone tired. Right to her core. She pulled her phone from her back pocket and called Skye.

"Hi Charly. How are you?"

"I'm fine. I'm sorry it's so late. How's Olive?"

"She's fine. We baked today. Worked with the horses. Shelby came and picked up Anders and Callie, but Olive opted to stay. She helped me make dinner, we ate. Lincoln came home after supper and he ate, then we sat and played Monopoly, which Olive won at. She's sound asleep in our spare bedroom. If you don't mind, just leave her here for the night. She's resting so peacefully."

Charly smiled. "Sounds like you wore her out. I'm so happy you all had a good day. Thank you again for watching her."

"Oh my goodness, it's our pleasure. Any sign of Haylie?"

"No. I so hoped we'd find her tonight, but no."

"You'll find her. I have faith in you all." Skye reassured.

She ended her call with Skye and turned to see Sam standing a few feet away.

"Everything okay?"

"Yeah. Sounds like Olive had a great day with Skye and Lincoln. She's staying there tonight."

"You good with that?"

Charly smiled at him. "I am. She needs fun and happiness in her life and I know she's safe as can be there. They practically have their place locked up like Fort Knox."

Sam laughed and she enjoyed watching him. His eyes crinkled in the corners and it was incredibly handsome on him. "It's a job hazard, babe."

She nodded and then felt a bit sheepish. What next?

Sam took her right hand in his and squeezed as he walked her to her car. They'd stopped at the station to check on Phillip Smith, answered a million questions, and wrote out reports. She'd then reported in to RAPTOR and they'd just now been released from all the work. It was well past midnight and it had been a long, damned day. Still, she wanted more. More with Sam.

He stopped walking with her as they reached her car and she stopped and faced him. His visage softened. His police face had been left at the door of the station. "Come home with me, Charly. Spend the night with me."

Her heart raced and her stomach struggled to contain the butterflies that erupted. She smiled at him and nodded.

"Yes." She couldn't say anything more. Just that one simple word.

He leaned down and kissed her lips softly. "Do you want to ride with me?"

"No. I'll follow you."

She wanted to say yes. But she wanted her independence and having her vehicle there was her way of having it. Sort of. She knew it was silly, but she still needed that.

"Okay. Follow me."

He kissed her again, then turned and walked to his car. She felt the loss of him as he walked away and she wanted to run after him, but instead, she took a deep breath and got into her car.

She followed behind Sam; he lived fairly close. And she knew where he lived because, shame on her, she'd researched him on the public records. She found his house and drove by a couple of times. Yes, she'd been that girl. She was intrigued with him and couldn't understand why this man was still single. She still wondered why.

Sam pulled into his garage, over to the far-left side, and she pulled in to the right, which was empty. Until now.

Those butterflies became active again and the thought of sleeping with Sam caused her body to flush red, the heat crawling up from her core. She felt like she'd just caught on fire and then the doubt set in. That was, until her door opened and Sam reached his hand in and waited for her to take it. He was always so chivalrous.

She lay her left hand in his and he steadied her as she stepped out of her SUV. The instant she stood in front of him, he bent his knees and pulled her to his body. Her feet left the ground and her arms wrapped around his shoulders, holding on to him. He kissed her lips and she happily kissed him back. When she wrapped her legs around his waist, he groaned and she swallowed it into her mouth. It vibrated through her and she felt the moisture gather between her legs. It was that sexy.

His hands slid down and cupped her ass and pulled her tighter to his body and she wanted him to be in her now.

At the entry of the house, he halted only a moment to close the garage door, then walked inside. He continued to kiss her, her lips, her neck, her cheek, back to her neck then her lips once again as he slowly walked through his house and to the bedroom. As he reached the bedroom, he continued through to a bathroom where he sat her on the counter. He backed up, "Take your clothes off, Charly. Your arm too."

"There's words you don't often hear." She said it jokingly and he chuckled.

Sam turned to the large glass-enclosed shower and turned the water on. Then he faced her and began stripping his clothes off. She wanted to watch him. So she did. He was magnificent. All of him.

He was muscular but not overly. Just more toned than anything, but it worked on him. When he unbuttoned his pants and lowered them to the floor, she saw the bulge stretching his boxer briefs tight and moisture gathered between her legs once again.

Then he lowered his briefs and she couldn't stop staring. Un-fucking-believable. Truly magnificent.

He walked over to her and pulled her shirt up and off of her. He then reached behind her, unsnapped her bra and tugged it forward, pulling it off her body. Sam lifted her off the counter to her feet and unbuttoned her jeans. She giggled and he responded. "You are taking too long."

He pushed her jeans and her panties down her legs and she stepped out of them. He looked at her and gruffly said, "I don't know how to remove your arm Charly."

She smiled and showed him. She pulled the skin-toned covering down so the connection was visible. Holding her arm away from her body, she twisted it slightly and pulled it from the metal pin at the end of her arm just below her elbow. She felt self-conscious as she lay her arm on the counter. She hadn't had sex with anyone since she'd lost her arm; this was the first time exposing herself. Exposing her left arm without her prosthetic was more humbling than showing him her body.

Sam reached out and softly ran his hand over her left arm from the shoulder down. When he reached the metal pin inserted into the end of her arm to support her prosthetic, he ran his fingers around the pin, then around the soft sensitive skin just above it and asked, "Why did they insert the pin instead of having the prosthetic slide over your arm?"

"At first that's what I had, but I kept having skin issues from it. My skin would peel, become sore and wearing the prosthetic became unbearable. Luckily, I was training for Operation Live Again, and the military paid for this type of prosthetic. I was a test patient, but it was to my benefit. At least this time."

Sam watched as his fingers then slid back up her arm, and over to her breasts. He softly cupped her left breast, then her right breast and watched as her nipples puckered.

"You're absolutely beautiful, Charly."

She huffed out a sound and he looked into her eyes. "It's true. One hundred percent."

He then took her right hand in his and walked them to the shower. The warmth enveloped her inside the shower, the hot water washed over her and to her complete surprise and utter amazement, Sam filled his hands with shower soap and began washing her body. His hands roamed all over her, touching her everywhere. Eliciting delicious and erotic feelings in her as he did.

He scooted her under the water to wet her hair, then filled his hands with shampoo, and worked them into her hair. She closed her eyes as he massaged her hair, her scalp, her temples, her nape. He seemed to enjoy it as much as she did. His voice was gruff when he said, "Rinse."

She smiled and stepped under the warm water as Sam then washed himself. She was slightly disappointed by that because she'd hoped she could wash him. She stopped his hands from running over his chest, "Let me."

"I don't know if I'll last."

She smiled, "You'll last."

Then she smoothed her right hand over his body. Right now, more than any time she could remember, she missed her left arm. She'd love to be able to run both of her hands over his amazing body. Feeling his skin under her fingertips, feeling the chest hairs so coarse and crisp under her fingers. It made her sad.

He leaned down and kissed her lips softly. "Why are you frowning?"

She shook her head. "Not now."

She let her right hand roam down to his cock, which was thick and long and ready for her. She fisted it in her hand and pumped him a few times, nice and slow and steady. A solid rhythm back and forth, back and forth. He began pushing into her hand and she heard his breathing change.

He stepped under the water to rinse the soap off his body.

She noticed a wooden seat at the back of the shower and she gently pushed him to the seat. He sat and she climbed up on top of him, positioned his cock at her entrance and slowly lowered herself down onto him. His head rested against the wall, his eyes closed briefly and he groaned as she filled herself with him. It took a few times, her lifting up and sliding down until he was fully inside of her but once he was, she stopped for just a moment to enjoy how she felt filled with his cock.

His hands cupped her ass once again and he lifted and lowered her, helping her to fuck him. They worked in unison, up and down, slowly at first, but it had been such a long time for her. She'd been thinking about Sam Bowers for months now. Dreaming about how he'd feel in her. Imagining the two of them together. In unison.

She increased the pace and both of them began to breathe in staccato. Then, he lifted his right hand to her mouth and she sucked his forefinger inside and swirled her tongue around and sucked as he pulled it from her mouth. Her eyes widened as his finger worked at the small opening in her ass, and as he slowly pushed his finger inside of her, she reared up then back down, pushing his finger in further. She sighed as she felt so full. His finger and his cock all at once. It was so freaking amazing.

He dipped his head and nipped at her throat, kissing his way up her neck and to her ear. She stopped raising and lowering herself to gyrate her hips back and forth, grinding against him giving her clit adequate pressure. His lips close to her ear he whispered, "Come, Charly. Let go."

It didn't take long after that. She ground against him a few more times and released a loud moan at the same time her body convulsed her orgasm. He waited for her to finish, his left hand rubbing her back while his right finger pushed in and out of her ass a few more times.

Once her orgasm had subsided, he pulled his finger from her ass, and with both hands he held her tightly and began pumping into her from his seated position. His strong legs able to push up into her which felt like nothing she'd ever felt. When he strained once more and groaned loudly, letting himself go, it was the first time she'd even thought about protection. They didn't use protection.

quick movement on the bed had Sam wide awake. His eyes opened and he saw Charly sitting up in bed.

"What's wrong?" His voice didn't sound like him.

"She was there. She was there—Haylie."

"Honey, what do you mean?"

Sam sat up now, and Charly turned to look into his eyes.

"Haylie had been at the house in Saginaw Village. The horses on the blanket and the horse magazine. Haylie loves horses. She wants to own a bunch of them one day."

Sam swallowed. "They likely moved her after Olive shot Harry."

"Where would they move her?"

Charly scrambled off the bed and disappeared into the bathroom. A minute later the toilet flushed, the water ran in the sink then Charly came out of the bathroom twisting her left arm onto the metal pin. She rolled the skin-colored rubber covering over her arm, then began dressing.

"Let me call Deacon and see if anyone in RAPTOR saw anything at the other houses."

Charly stopped him, "I'll call Deac. You call the station and see if shithead is ready to talk."

She seemed frantic and full of energy. Sam got out of bed and walked to her. Pulling her to him for a moment, he hugged her close then whispered, "Good morning, Charly."

She relaxed, her face tilted up to his and she smiled. "I'm sorry. Good morning. I guess I was so tired last night I didn't put two and two together. I didn't mean to scare you awake this morning."

He bent down and kissed her. He just meant it to be a peck, but then his lips softened and she kissed him back and, well, he was just a man after all. And she was a gorgeous, vivacious woman.

When he pulled back a bit, he ran the back of his fore-finger over the slight bruise on her cheek under her eye. "I'm sorry about this."

She smiled, "Babe, it's a job hazard."

He chuckled then. She was right. "One more thing. We didn't use protection yesterday."

"I know." She took a deep breath and looked up at him. "I'm clean. I actually haven't had sex in over three and a half years to be honest."

His eyes widened. "You've got to be kidding me."

"No. Since this." She lifted her left arm.

He swallowed. He couldn't say it had been that long, but he knew he was clean. "I'm clean too." Then he swallowed and hoped she wouldn't ask how long it had been for him. Not now.

"Okay. We'll be more careful in the future."

"Deal."

Charly sat in the chair in the corner and pulled her shoes on and Sam pulled clean clothes from his dresser and began dressing.

"I don't suppose you have an extra toothbrush laying around?" Charly asked.

Sam chuckled. "Actually, I have several." Her brow furrowed and he laughed. He walked to the bathroom and opened a drawer alongside the sink.

"Take your pick." There were around ten brand new toothbrushes laying in the drawer and an equal number of tiny tubes of toothpaste.

"Please don't tell me you keep these around because you have so many female callers."

He laughed. "No, Charly, I don't have female callers." He leaned against the counter and crossed his arms. "Every time I go to the dentist for a cleaning, I get a brand-new toothbrush and a tube of toothpaste with a small floss in a goodie bag. I don't use that kind of toothbrush, so I just toss them all in here."

He pointed to the counter where his electric toothbrush sat and she nodded.

"Why are you single, Sam Bowers?"

His face scrunched at the question and the memories. Most of them bad.

"I'm divorced. She couldn't take my job. My hours are unpredictable and she wanted more. Steady. Regular. I couldn't offer that."

Charly stepped into his space. Her left arm reached up and softly brushed down his cheek. He could hear the miniature motors running as her fingers opened and closed. Her eyes were watching as her left hand mimicked the gentle lover's motion. Then her eyes shifted to his. "I so wish I could feel with this hand. I wanted it so badly last night."

"Is that why you frowned when we were in the shower?"

She only nodded and he watched the wistfulness in her expression.

"You make up for it in other ways, you know."

She smiled. "Like how?"

"Like, with your right hand..." He lifted her right hand to his lips and kissed her fingers. "You caressed me so completely. Like you were trying to memorize how I felt under your touch. Your expression said it all. You touched everywhere you could." He then lifted her left hand and kissed her fingers. "You felt like no other. Ever. Your body fits mine. You move with purpose. You showed me without words how much you wanted me. You did it without fake platitudes of promise. You did it with all that is you, Charlesia Sampson."

Her eyes glistened with moisture and she blinked rapidly. He pulled her into him, his legs opening so she could stand between them. He bent down and kissed her lips again. This time with purpose. With need. With wanting. He hoped he could convey to her with his body how much he wanted her. It was a feeling he'd never had before. Even when he'd first met his ex. This was wholly different. Maybe because he'd matured. Maybe because he had a better understanding of life and how fleeting it was. And, maybe it was because Charlesia Sampson was his soul mate. Maybe it was all of that.

Her right hand slid into his hair at the back of his head and her fingers massaged his head as her lips fit against his. Their tongues danced together, each eager to taste more of the other. Their breathing grew ragged, each fighting the urge to pull away to breathe and not wanting to break contact. His cock thickened and he enjoyed how she moved against it, even though they both wore clothing.

She pulled back slightly, her eyes opening in a dreamy soft expression. The crisp blue reminded him of a new spring sky, clear, fresh, and full of promise. She was stunning.

They held each other's gaze for a long time; neither wanted to break the spell that had just been cast over them. He opened his mouth to tell her. But instead he pulled her into a hug and held on. He was scared to take that next step. He thought she felt the same, but what if she didn't?

27

C harly snapped pictures of the blanket and the magazine. She'd ask Olive if they were Haylie's. She felt in her heart they were close.

Her phone rang and she answered quickly.

"Charly here."

"Hey Charly, it's Piper."

"Hey Pipes, what's up?"

"So, Falcon and Creed called with some interesting news."

Charly sat on the edge of the little bed. "Okay."

"So the owner of the land where the coordinates led allowed them to do some digging. They found two bodies buried out there. There's a coroner, and heavy equipment out there now digging up more in the area. The coroner will take the bodies to his lab and perform DNA tests and try to identify them."

"Holy crap. Do you know if they are adults or kids?"

"They're adults. It was the first thing I asked. Great minds."

"Yeah. Thanks Pipes. I appreciate being kept up to speed on it."

"How are things going there?"

Charly looked at the blanket with the horses and lay her hand on it. "I found a blanket with horses on it. Haylie loves horses. I took a picture of it and I'll show Olive when I see her later. I think it's Haylie's. She isn't here, but I believe she was. Sam thinks she was probably moved after Olive shot Harry. It probably shook things up here."

"Good work, Charly. You're getting close. You'll have Haylie home in no time."

"Wherever that is."

Piper was quiet for a moment. Then she asked, "Truly, I know you have a strong connection with Olive, but do you really see yourself raising her? And Haylie? How would that work, Charly?"

Charly's eyes filled with moisture and she stared down at the blanket watching as it wavered in front of her. "I honestly don't know how it could work. But I feel responsible that I didn't follow up with Olive before and look what's happened to her. I just can't let that happen again. You know?"

"Yeah. I get it. Diego, Emmy, and Van have been torn up about it too."

"We let her down, Pipes."

"No we didn't. We assumed social services would do their jobs."

"Yeah. We know what a mistake that was." Charly swiped at her eyes and sniffed. "Thanks for keeping me informed Pipes. We're still at the house in Saginaw Village, searching for evidence. We've found a shit ton of ammo tucked in closets, under the floorboards, and in false bottoms of dresser drawers, it's unreal. There are some guns too."

"Nice work. Keep it up, Charly. I'll see you when you get back."

The line went dead and Charly tapped her phone to end the call. She looked up to see Sam watching her from the doorway.

"You okay?" He walked into the room and stared down at her.

She stood and took a deep breath. "Yeah. Piper called. They found two bodies buried out in the field where the coordinates you found led them. They have authorities there now and are exhuming the bodies and digging for more."

"Wow. This is getting pretty deep."

"Yeah. Who do you think it could be?"

He took a deep breath. "I don't know. I just got a call from Captain Peters. We can't get a warrant for the cigar store or the house in Paxton. No evidence that anything happened there. So I'm heading back to the station to go through the notebooks we found at the house in Lynyrd."

Charly nodded. "Okay. I'm going out to Skye and Lincoln's to see Olive and make sure she's doing alright. I'll show her the pictures of the blanket and the magazine and see if she can confirm that these are Haylie's. If they are, when the station is finished with them, can Olive have them until we find Haylie?"

Sam smiled softly, stepped in, and wrapped his arms around her. "I'll see what I can do."

She hugged him back. They stood like that for a while. It felt good. He felt good. Like they were supposed to be together. Her heart hurt less when she was with Sam.

He squeezed her then stepped back. "I gotta run, babe. Are you okay?"

"Yeah. I'll see you later?" It was a question. She didn't know where they went from here. There was no conversation about being exclusive, or seeing each other more, or anything future wise. A slight panic rolled through her body as she thought about Sam not wanting to spend time with her anymore. She hated that she felt so vulnerable. Charly needed her mojo back, and fast.

"Absolutely. Why don't you let me know what your status is later? If you have Olive and need to stay with her tonight, I understand. If the three of us can do something, that works too. If you don't have Olive and want to be with me, I'd love that."

Her cheeks heated thinking about his last sentence. She wanted to be with him for certain. "I'll call you in a while. Before I see about Olive, I'm driving out to the Paxton house and taking pictures of it. Then the cigar store. I want to show all of them to Olive and see if she's been to any of them and if she can tell me anything that will help us figure out where Haylie is."

He kissed her forehead. "You're amazing, Charly."

The expression on his face told her what she needed to know. He wanted to be with her and, just maybe he admired her? That'd be something, 'cause she admired the shit out of Sam Bowers. She listened to his steps as he descended to the living room and out the back door, until she couldn't hear him anymore.

Charly looked around. There was nothing else she could do here. The police were packing things up and she needed to stay out of the way. She looked wistfully at the blanket and magazine and had started to leave when her phone rang.

"Charly."

"Babe." Sam's voice was deep and gravelly. "Captain said you can take the blanket and magazine if you make sure Ty and Eydie have pictures of it first."

"You called him?"

"Yeah. In case you can't tell, I kinda have a soft spot for you."

"It wasn't soft last night." She teased.

His voice deepened. "It isn't soft now either."

He ended the call and she had to sit back down for a minute as her knees shook and her panties dampened. Holy shit, that was H-O-T.

28

F our hours later Sam was still sitting at the station, pouring over smelly nicotine-infused notebooks full of scrawling handwriting and a myriad of notes and ledger type entries.

His head ached and his nostrils were assaulted anew with every turn of the page. Then, he'd gotten lucky when a loose page fell out of the notebook as he was leafing through and found the name of A. Rodinger, on a paystub. The address on the stub was in Lynyrd Station and, needing a break from the stench and sedentary day, Sam decided to take a ride.

On the way over to A. Rodinger's place, Sam formulated what he'd say to the man to get him to open up. His skills might just be tested today. Then again, if he no longer worked there, maybe he'd be open to spilling some secrets, if there were any.

Sam pulled into the driveway and looked around. This section of town was filled with homes built in the seventies, mostly single-story, but all well-kept and friendly looking. The neighbors all had pretty flowers growing in the yards and around the houses and all of the homes were made of either brick or a stone of some sort.

Feeling encouraged, Sam got out of his car and walked to the front door. He rang the doorbell and waited. The door opened and a lady in her early sixties answered the door. She was trim, her hair neatly cut and colored in a reddish-brown tint. She wore glasses with tortoise shell frames and a smile on her face.

"Hello. May I help you?"

"Are you Mrs. Rodinger?"

"Yes sir. My name is Alice."

Sam halted for a moment. He assumed A. Rodinger was a male, now he wondered if his assumption was incorrect. "Mrs. Rodinger, did your husband work at the W. Smith Cigar and Tobacco Store?"

Her smile faded as she looked into Sam's eyes. "Who needs to know this?"

"I do." He held his hand out with his business card. "My name is Sam Bowers and I'm a detective with the Lynyrd Station Police Department. If Mr. Rodinger is home, I do need to speak with him."

Her eyes welled with tears and her voice cracked when she asked, "Is he in trouble Mr. Bowers?"

Sam smiled at her. "No ma'am. But I am hoping he can help me solve a mystery."

A man appeared behind Mrs. Rodinger. He was tall, about six foot two, not as tall as Sam and certainly much thinner. Reedy was the first thing Sam thought of as a way to describe him. Tall and reedy.

"What's going on here?"

Alice turned to her husband and handed him Sam's business card. Sam quickly spoke. "Mr. Rodinger, I'm investigating the murder of Harry Smith and some of the illegal guns and ammunition we found in the house. Your check stub fell out of a notebook as I was searching through the contents and I wondered if you'd be so kind as to talk to me to perhaps clear up some of the mysteries surrounding the Smiths."

Mr. Rodinger looked at his wife and gently patted her on the shoulder. "It's alright, Alice honey. Maybe you can make us some tea. We've expected this visit for years now."

Alice nodded and Mr. Rodinger opened the door for Sam to step inside.

The living room was neat and tidy. A gray sofa and loveseat formed a forty-five-degree angle along two of the walls. A white coffee table sat in front of the sofa with a small bowl of fresh flowers in the middle and a remote control on the end of it. A television hung on the wall opposite the sofa and two white end tables were positioned on either side of the love seat. Nothing out of place. Family pictures of the Rodingers hung on the walls; it looked as though they had three children and a few grandchildren.

Mr. Rodinger held his hand out to Sam. "My name is Allan."

Sam took his hand and firmly shook, receiving a nice firm handshake in return. This was a man used to making an impression.

"Nice to meet you Mr. Rodinger. Sam Bowers."

Once they'd finished their greeting, Allan motioned to the sofa and love seat, "Let's have a seat, shall we? I think we'll be here a while."

Sam was surprised at his statement and decided to record their conversation if allowed.

Allan sat at the end of the sofa, closest to the love seat and Sam sat at the end of the love seat, close to Allan.

"I'd like to record our conversation if you don't mind."

"Not at all. I figure it'll protect me in the long run."

"That's an interesting statement."

"I think you'll be enlightened quite a bit, Detective Bowers."

"Call me Sam."

Allan nodded and Alice brought them each a glass of iced tea and set them on coasters on the coffee table, then quietly left the room.

Allan watched quietly as Sam set up his phone on the table with the recorder running.

Sam then folded his hands together between his knees and looked at Mr. Rodinger. Allan.

Allan started without prompting. "I used to work for William Smith in the tobacco store. I left there about eight years ago now. It was not amicable. I'm telling you all of this because I've been diagnosed with pancreatic cancer. Terminal. I'm happy to unburden myself to you to protect Alice once I'm gone. Those Smiths are bad news."

"I'm sorry to hear of your health issues, Allan."

Allan raised his hand in the air as if to say, don't bother. He'd resigned himself to his fate. He continued. "I witnessed Howie Smith killing a man about nine years ago. He killed him in the tobacco store, late at night. His name was Randy Delhart. Randy had found out that the Smiths were selling young kids. It was by accident that he saw Howie Smith dropping off a younger boy and girl and accepting money for them. Randy stormed into the store and told Smith he was going to report him; that he was lower than low and scum of the earth. Howie shot him. I was there; I hid around the corner in the storeroom so he wouldn't see me and watched the whole thing happen. Nick Scott was there too. He and Howie were good friends. Howie had Nick help him load Delhart's body into the truck and they took him away. Later, Nick was scared and needed to talk to someone. He told me where they buried Delhart. I went out there with Nick the following day and wrote the coordinates down. After a couple of months, Nick was struggling, shaking, couldn't sleep. He tried talking to Howie about what he'd done. Said Delhart's widow deserved to know what happened. Howie killed him too. When Nick went missing, I drove back out to where Delhart was buried and saw another fresh grave alongside his. I knew what happened. When Howie wasn't paying attention, I took the gun and hid it in the wall in the basement of the cigar store. I cemented over the area and piled boxes in front of it. Howie was too lazy to ever look for it and he'd never go in the basement at the store to search."

"How did the coordinates get written inside the floorboards of the Harry Smith house?" Sam asked.

"I did it. It was my way of keeping any evidence away from my family and hiding it right under their thieving disgusting faces. I would often be asked to deliver boxes to one of the houses. I went there one day and no one was around. I felt that the floorboards were loose and lifted them. I found the guns and knew what they'd been having me deliver. I wrote the coordinates of the bodies inside the floor joists and quit working there. I told William I never wanted to see any of them again. We fought and he threatened that if I ever told anyone, he'd come after my family. That's why I never said anything. I told Alice I'd only say something if someone ever asked." He leaned forward and smiled. "I thought you'd never get here."

Sam smiled at Allan and nodded. "I almost didn't. If it hadn't been for that check stub, I may not have."

Allan nodded. "I wrote it all out and asked Alice to deliver it to the police after I died. Just in case."

Allan took a sip of his tea. Sam did the same.

"Do you know where or who they're selling the kids to?"

"No. If you can search the tobacco store, I'm sure there will be a wealth of information there. William did all his shady business upstairs."

"Did you ever see kids around?"

"Nope. Until the night Randy was killed, I never knew anything bad was happening there. I knew that family wasn't right. There were secrets and weird conversations but nothing ever told me anything like that was happening."

"How about the guns? Do you know where they were getting them and who they were selling them to?"

"No. I'm sorry Sam. I didn't want anything to do with that business and I was afraid if I did too much digging, my family would be in danger. Taking the gun and going out to where the bodies were buried were the bravest things I've ever done." His voice grew soft. "And, I'm afraid I wasn't really that brave at all. It's kept me awake at night wondering about the kids. How many of them were there? What happened to them?"

Sam nodded. "I understand." He took another drink of his tea. "Will you tell me exactly where I can find the gun?"

Allan nodded. "I can take you right to it."

Sam stopped the recording. "I'll need to get a search warrant first. Let me call my captain and get him working on it."

29

C harly drove up to Skye and Lincoln Winters' house and smiled when she saw Olive and Skye outside near the corral feeding the horses.

Olive looked up and waved wildly when she saw Charly, the biggest smile on her face Charly had ever seen. Charly's heart raced just seeing the difference in Olive. Walking as quickly as she could toward Olive, she could feel the peace here. It was like the air changed. At the base of Lynyrd Station on the Hill Mountain, their house was nestled along the river at the back, the sound of the water flowing was the perfect background sound. The horse corral sat to the right of the house where two horses enjoyed their hay, tails swishing, and their ears flicking back and forth, listening for everything. The barn at the back of the corral looked brand new, straight and solid and neat as could be. It was the most impressive scenery she'd ever seen. It truly was a slice of heaven out here.

Olive ducked under the fencing and ran to her and Charly knelt down to receive her hug. It felt so good. It was the first time Olive had hugged her on her own. Tears sprang to Charly's eyes and she held Olive for as long as the young girl would let her. Skye waved at Charly as she opened the gate and closed it again, making her way toward them.

Skye Winters was a beautiful woman. Tall and thin with long blond hair and the bluest eyes she'd ever seen. She had a regal, sophisticated air about her but Charly knew she was more down to earth than anyone. She wore blue jeans tucked into cowboy boots and a loose-fitting t-shirt tucked into her jeans. Her gorgeous hair blew in the breeze that swirled around them.

"Hi Charly. How are you?" Skye smiled as she approached. Olive released Charly and she stood to hug Skye.

"I'm good. How are you?"

"I'm good," she said, echoing Charly's words. "We've been having a grand time here."

Olive started chatting. "It's just great here, Charly. Come and see the horses. They're so awesome. They eat right from my hand and they let me ride them. And they watch me while I help fill the water in the tuff."

Skye laughed. "Trough."

Olive nodded. "Trough."

Charly laughed at Olive's exuberance and followed behind her as the little girl ran to the corral where the two horses stood grazing.

Olive ducked under the fence and stood next to the two horses as they ate.

"This is Blue Zeus," she patted the first horse on the side. Blue Zeus nodded his head as if acknowledging her, then Olive walked way behind the horses and to the side of the second one eating its hay and said, "This one is Huckleberry."

Huckleberry continued to eat as if no one was watching him. Olive walked back to the corral fence where Charly stood and whispered, "I like riding Huckleberry the best, he goes slower."

As if on cue, Huckleberry pulled a mouthful of hay from a cube and shook it. Olive hooted in delight, which made Skye and Charly laugh.

Olive climbed up on the fence and looked down at Charly. "Do I have to go back? I wanted to spend more time with Huckleberry."

Charly smiled at her and Skye responded. "It's fine with me, Charly. We were going to go for a ride in a little while then make Lincoln and ourselves some lunch. Would you like to join us?"

Charly smiled at Skye and watched her eyes. She looked at Olive and smiled. It was a warm loving smile and Charly felt their connection.

"I don't need to stay for lunch but I would like to have a little chat if we could. Please."

Skye nodded. "Of course. Do you mean you and Olive, or both of us?"

"Actually, if we all could go in and chat, I'd appreciate it."

"Okay." Skye nodded.

Olive jumped down from the fence and for the first time Charly noticed she was wearing jeans and cowboy boots like Skye.

"Where did you get those cute boots, Olive?"

"Skye and Lincoln bought them. We went shopping yesterday afternoon. I got new jeans and t-shirts and some bibs." Olive looked at Skye. "Is that how you say it?"

Skye laughed. "Yes. Bib overalls. For doing chores."

Olive nodded. "Chores means we feed the horses."

Charly giggled and nodded. She then looked at Skye. "I have something to grab from my car, I'll be right in."

"Okay. We'll get some tea ready for all of us."

Charly diverted from their path and walked back to her car. She pulled the neatly folded blanket and magazine from the front passenger seat and waited until Skye and Olive had gone inside. She swallowed because she wasn't sure how Olive would handle this and she sure seemed happy here. She hoped having Skye with her would be a help in receiving the news. While not bad news, she still hadn't found Haylie and so it was, maybe, bittersweet.

After the door to the house closed, Charly took a deep breath and walked to the house, trying hard to tamp down the roiling in her stomach.

Once she reached the door she hesitated because she didn't know if she should knock on the door or just go in. Skye looked over and waved her in, stopping her debate.

Charly entered the house and instantly felt at home. Everything was just like you'd imagine a western decorated home to be. Woods and wood-toned furniture, leather sofas in the living room, which could be seen from the kitchen, homey things hanging on the walls. All of it. Charly couldn't offer Olive anything like this. This was a home. Charly lived at the compound which was very nice, but not a real home like this.

Skye looked over at Charly, then her eyes dropped to the blanket she carried and worry creased her brow.

Charly shook her head but walked to the table and lay the blanket and magazine on top then looked at Olive.

"Olive, honey, is this Haylie's blanket?"

Olive walked to the table and lay her hand on the top of the blanket and smoothed her fingers over the top. Tears tracked down her cheeks as she simply caressed the blanket. Her head nodded.

"How about this magazine? Do you recognize it?" Charly asked softly.

Olive nodded again. "Did you find her?"

Charly shook her head. "No honey, we didn't. But we believe we're really close."

"She'll be so sad without her blanket."

Charly knelt down and rubbed Olive's back with her right hand. "As soon as we find her, we'll give Haylie her blanket back. Would you like to keep it for her until then?"

"Yeah."

Skye set three glasses of iced tea down, then retrieved the cheese and crackers she'd readied. Skye quietly sat at the table and lay her hand over Olive's on the blanket. "Charly and her coworkers are the best in the world at finding lost people. They'll find Haylie, Olive. I have faith in them."

Olive nodded her head then stepped over and hugged Skye.

Charly swallowed the lump in her throat, then sat across the table from Skye and watched her console Olive. She whispered something in Olive's ear and smoothed her hand over Olive's back and before long, Olive climbed up in Skye's lap and sat still as could be.

Charly smiled. Skye was good with her.

30

S am drove to the tobacco store with Allan Rodinger in his car; both were somber. Allan was resigned to unload all of his secrets so he could rest in peace. That's what he told Sam.

Alice worried that the Smiths would find out Allan had hidden evidence and would come after her or their children. Sam said he'd see what he could do to protect her.

Sam turned onto the street where the W. Smith Cigar and Tobacco store still stood. A sad looking building, as no upkeep had been done on the store in years.

"Why did they stop keeping the store up? It was a great cover and a way for them to launder their illegal money," he said, mostly to himself, but Allan heard him.

"They bought a car wash in Paxton and are funneling their money through there."

"We didn't find any evidence of that."

Allan looked over at him. "That, I'm sure, is by design. I heard them whispering about it before I quit the store. They bought things under the LLC TamCo. Tammy was all proud that her name was sort of on something. They used a lawyer to be the registered agent at the time. He's a judge now. Judge Kissinger."

Sam recalled his conversation yesterday with Richie Reynolds. He'd insinuated that Judge Kissinger was on the take.

Sam pulled to the curb in front of the tobacco store; two squad cars were parked on the other side of the street. Allan took a deep breath and sighed. "Here goes."

Allan unbuckled his seatbelt and opened the door. Sam did the same. As Sam stepped up onto the sidewalk an old man walked out of the storefront. His steps were labored and slow. His right hand held a cane to assist his steps, his left hand tucked in his front trouser pocket.

His sallow skin was partially covered by a white beard, which was yellowed from years of smoking.

Allan nodded at him, but said nothing.

Sam stepped forward and handed him the warrant he'd obtained. "Mr. Smith..."

The older man simply glared at Mr. Rodinger, eyes full of malice, but said nothing. "Mr. Smith, this is a search warrant for the premises. You'll need to stay outside here with an officer while we search."

William Smith simply gazed at Allan Rodinger, glared actually, but said nothing. He also refused to take the search warrant, so Sam walked past him with the warrant in his hand, deciding to leave it inside. Allan followed him without a word.

Entering the store was like stepping back in time. Nothing had changed here since Sam's uncle had brought him here as a boy. Same old scarred wooden counter with the glass front and top. Same old signs on the wall. The old wooden Cigar Store Indian, which had been a popular advertising tool back in the day, stood in the corner, now covered in dust. Most of the shelves were empty now; no one had bothered to clean the store or completely close it down. Anything still in stock was long stale and unusable.

Sam turned to Allan, "Show me where you hid the gun."

Allan nodded and walked behind the wooden counter. He stopped before a door cut in the floor. "I won't be able to lift this anymore. I don't have much in the way of strength these days."

Sam stepped past him and pulled on a latch carved into the trap door and lifted it. It was tricky to open; you had to then walk along a narrow strip of floor to lay the opened door onto the other side of the floor. That's how old the building was.

Once he had the door secured on the other side, Allan backed down the steep stairs, holding on to the shaking railing as he went. "Be careful coming down Sam. Not to be rude, but you're a far sight bigger than I am."

Sam only chuckled. He knew his size.

As Allan descended, he flipped a switch to turn on the light. At the bottom of the steps, Allan waited for Sam, then looked around the basement.

"It all looks exactly the same as it did the last time I was down here."

"Let's hope everything is still right where you put it."

Allan nodded and walked to the shelves along the wall to his left. He moved some dank, horrible-smelling boxes, the dust thick on top, and Allan shook his head.

"Such waste. They just left this stuff down here to rot."

"It's likely only pennies compared to the money they're making in illegal arms and child trafficking."

Allan spit on the floor in disgust and shook his head. "I've prayed and prayed to the Lord for forgiveness. That's what scares me most these days. That I won't be forgiven."

"If you've prayed to the Lord and confessed, I have no doubt you'll be saved in the end, Allan."

Once they'd moved several boxes, Allan showed Sam what needed to be done next. "This shelf lifts off right here." He pointed to the shelf and the wooden blocks Allan had screwed into the braces to let the shelf rest.

Sam lifted it off and Allan walked over to a metal container on the opposite side of the room, lifted the lid and pulled out some rags.

"At least they left everything where it had been."

Allan walked to the space the lifted shelf had concealed and began wiping at the stone wall behind it. After a few swipes of the rag Sam could see the course texture of where he'd cemented a few rocks back in place.

"There was a loose rock here. I pulled the rock out, tucked the gun in a metal container we received our raw tobacco in and pushed it inside the wall. Then I hit the back of the rock with a hammer to break enough off of it that it would fit back into the wall and conceal the gun. Then I cemented it in."

"Why did you cement all around all of this section of rocks?"

"So it wouldn't be noticeable."

Sam nodded. Allan was a smart old fella.

Ty Anderson made his way down the steps carrying a hammer, a pry bar, and miscellaneous other tools.

"Right here, Ty." Sam pointed to the rock Allan had pointed out. Ty placed the end of the pry bar into the seam around the rock and hit the end of it with the hammer. After a few hard taps, the cement began falling off in large clumps. Allan stood back and watched them work, and Sam watched Ty and Allan in equal increments of time. Soon the rock was loose and Ty pulled it free from its place in the wall.

Sam pulled a flashlight from his pocket and shined it into the hole in the wall. There was indeed a cigar box tucked inside and Sam nodded at Ty to pull it out.

It didn't come out nice and easy, but it did come out eventually, and Ty handed the box to Sam. Sam held it like it was a precious jewel. He looked over at Allan, who had tears in his eyes, but he said nothing, he just nodded once.

"Anything I need to know about this box before I open it, Allan?"

C harly got out of her shower, changed into clean clothes, dried her hair, and left her apartment to head down to the conference room. She needed to do some internet searching.

Piper greeted her from the bank of computers as she entered the conference room.

"Hey, long time no see. Where were you last night?" Piper's grin and her high blond ponytail made her look like a teenager.

Charly smiled even as her cheeks flushed pink. "Never mind."

Piper giggled and stood. From the careful way she moved today, Charly suspected the shrapnel lodged in her back was giving Piper some trouble. Although it was hard to tell. She moved slowly when in pain, but also out of caution even when she wasn't in pain. After she'd gotten her balance and knew she wouldn't make any false steps,

Piper walked to the table that served as their conference table.

"Caiden and I were in contact with the coroner's office. The bodies are both male, both in their forties or early fifties, both shot at close range based on the damage to the clothing they still had on them. The coroner wouldn't give us any more information, said we had to get that from the police department. Emmy is on the phone with them now."

"Okay. Thanks, Pipes. Olive looked at the pictures of the house in Paxton and the cigar store. She'd been at the house but not the cigar store. "I'm here to talk to Emmy about going into the house in Paxton. I think I'm going to need backup for that one. By now the Smiths will know we're getting close and they may have assistance in protecting their disgusting illegal operations."

"I'm glad you aren't going in alone, Charly."

"Not this time. Are Falcon or Creed back from finding dead bodies?"

"Yeah, they're both taking showers."

"Good."

Charly stood to walk over to her computer when Piper said, "Deacon told me about you and Sam."

Charly stopped; her face burned hot and her throat dried almost instantly.

"I told him not to say anything."

Piper laughed. "You know he doesn't listen when it comes to something like that. So...tell me. Are you two a thing now?"

Charly sat back down, she turned in her chair and looked into Piper's eyes. "I don't know. I think so. But we haven't had the conversation."

"Okay."

Piper stood and waited for her body to catch up with her. "Are you happy?"

Charly smiled and felt her face grow hot once more. "Yes."

Piper stepped away. "That's all that matters."

Charly walked to her computer and shook the mouse to wake it up.

Piper said from across the room, "Deacon and I managed to piece together a floor plan of the house in Paxton by locating the builder and asking for the blueprints or at the very least, a drawing of the layout of the house. We said we wanted to build one like it. They're in the file."

"Thanks Pipes." Charly planned to study it and then work on a plan until Creed and Falcon came back down.

Her phone chimed a text and she looked down to see Skye Winters' name. Opening the text it said, "Olive is asking if she can stay the night again. Lincoln and I love having her."

Charly smiled and took a deep breath. She was going to have to let Olive go one of these days, not completely, but emotionally, and Skye and Lincoln were good to her. "As long as you don't mind and she's happy, that's all that matters. She has a doctor's appointment tomorrow at ten. Can you take her?"

The three dots bounced as Skye texted back. "Absolutely. Send me the address and the paperwork allowing me to be there with her."

Charly pulled up the paperwork and sent it over via email along with the doctor's appointment location and time. She then pulled up the layout of the Paxton house and, fighting the urge to run out and see Olive again, she sent it over to Skye. "Would you ask Olive if she can tell us what rooms they put the kids in in this house? Making a plan here."

Falcon Montgomery walked into the conference room and sat in a chair to her left.

"So, babe, what's happening in your investigation?"

"Shut up, Falcon."

He laughed, his dark eyes sparkling with glee. He was handsome, all of the guys here were, but she'd never had a crush on any of them. They were all like siblings or brothers and sisters in arms, which struck her as weird. The first time she'd seen Sam, she couldn't stop thinking about him. Couldn't stop wondering about him. Such a visceral reaction to someone you've never met when she worked with all these badass, buff men. She shook her head.

Falcon stopped laughing and lowered his voice. "In all honesty, Sam is a great guy. My dad has known him since he came here a couple of years ago. Dad and Rory are friends, have been since high school and Rory thinks the world of Sam."

Charly put her hand on his. "Thanks Falcon. It's new. I'm not sure where it will go, so there's that."

"Fair enough."

"So, purposely changing the subject: I'm going out to the house in Paxton as soon as it gets dark. I'd love it if you and Creed joined me. I don't know what to expect, but they know we're picking away at them now and they'll be on guard. Also, they'll be moving the kids tonight if they have any. They aren't going to risk keeping them anyplace we can find."

"Okay, I agree with you. Did you talk to Emmy?"

The door opened and Emmy walked into the room. "I'll talk with her right now."

"Talk to me about what?" Emmy was usually all business.

"I want to go to the house in Paxton tonight and I'd like Falcon and Creed to come with me."

"Solid idea. I just got off the phone with Captain Peters. They've identified the bodies, in large part because of a former employee that Sam Bowers is working with today."

At the mention of Sam's name, Charly's heart fluttered and her face heated. She wondered how long it would take to not have this kind of reaction to just his name.

32

Sam took Allan home, thanked him for helping them out and left. At the police station, he walked into his office, tired as hell, and hungry. It was well past six in the evening and after thinking about it, he hadn't eaten lunch or supper.

He pulled his cell phone from his pocket and called Charly. He wanted to see her. He wanted to tell her about his day, which also might help her find Haylie. And, he just wanted to hold her in his arms.

"Hi, Sam. How'd your day go?" His heart reacted to her voice and he imagined what she looked like talking to him.

He smiled as he replied. "It was interesting. How was your day?"

"Interesting. Also, a bit depressing."

"Yeah. Did you eat supper?"

"No. You?"

"No. Can I pick you up? We'll go out."

"Yes but only for a while. I'm going out to the Paxton house with Falcon and Creed when it gets dark. I think Haylie's there, and I want to get there before they move her."

Sam sat back in his chair. He had to really stop himself from what he wanted to ask. Why did she have to go? Would she be careful? Can I come with you?

Instead, he said, "Okay. Well, let's have a quick dinner, then I'll take you to Paxton."

"You sure you want to come? It may not be all 'inside the lines' type of work. I'm getting Haylie back. I don't care what I have to do."

Sam swallowed. "I know. I do. And another set of hands and eyes can't hurt."

She was silent for a moment and he sighed in relief when she finally responded. "Okay."

"Just out of curiosity, why don't you think they moved Haylie during the day? Like this afternoon?"

"Olive said they always moved them at night. Easier to conceal themselves. The kids were scared to run at night and even though they know we're on to them, we've had operatives watching the house, there's been no movement."

"Okay. Then I'll be there in about fifteen minutes."

"I'll meet you out front."

The line went dead and Sam stared out the window of his office. Should he tell Captain Peters he was going out there? He wasn't going in his official capacity, so he heaved his tired body from his chair and walked out of the building.

Just as he reached his car, Captain Peters called from the door of the building. "Sam."

Sam turned and strode back to speak to his boss, feeling a bit uneasy. He almost felt like he was caught in a lie.

"Hey Captain."

"I just wanted you to know that the bodies have been identified as Nick Scott and Randy Delhart, thanks to you and Mr. Rodinger. DNA for full confirmation is still a couple of weeks out, but we pulled up the reports of the missing men and the descriptions of what they were wearing when they were last seen. With dental records, we're confident in the preliminary identifications."

Sam nodded. "Thanks Cap. What's going to happen to Allan Rodinger?"

"I'll talk to the DA tomorrow. He didn't come forward about two murders. He hid a murder weapon. There could be obstruction charges, but in light of his health condition, it really would be a waste to spend any time prosecuting him. I'll see what I can do."

"Thank you. He did save us a lot of time in helping us out. How long are you able to hold William Smith?"

"A couple of days. We're still finding evidence at the tobacco store. And I think we can argue he's a flight risk. Also, thanks to you finding all the books at the tobacco store and the house, we've found the accounting of all the kids they've kidnapped or purchased and resold. It's a multi-million-dollar business. It's staggering."

"That it is. Is Haylie Tomm's name in that notebook?"

"You're welcome to come and take a look at it."

Captain Peters turned and walked to his office, Sam followed closely behind. "The book's here." He pointed to a box of evidence sitting on his desk.

Sam pulled the notebook out with shaking fingers. Sitting in a chair on the opposite side of Captain Peters' desk, he opened the book to the back and the last entries. Skimming down the pages he saw her name. 'Haylie Tomms - n/k/a Susan Jackson - v. Birthdate 10/24/2010. $80,000.00.'

Sam read the numbers and his mouth dropped open. Then he looked at the other names. All changed to names that were so common in the English language. Brian, Susan, Tracy, Nancy, Shelly. All of them had birthdates by them. He looked closely at the dates, then his blood ran cold.

Each of the kids was kept until they were twelve years old, then sold. Haylie would be twelve in a month.

He told his captain what he saw and Captain Peters' jaw tightened. They looked at the names and numbers together and Captain asked, "What does the V stand for? Some of them have an N by them."

Sam looked back at the names and noticed a couple of things. The names with the V got more money. Then he saw a familiar name—Eleese.

He picked up his phone and dialed Charly once again.

"Hey there, are you here already?"

"No, not yet. Charly, what did Olive say about Eleese?"

"Aah, she said she had a baby."

Eleese's name had a N by it. She'd also been sold for only $25,000. The initials after payment were JFP.

"Okay. I'll be right there."

"Is everything alright?"

Sam took a deep breath and exhaled slowly. "Yeah. We'll talk about it when I get there."

Sam stood. "May I share these with RAPTOR, Captain?"

"Of course. If it'll help them in finding some of those kids, absolutely."

Sam made copies of several of the pages of the book. Enough to show Charly some of the last couple of years. Then he laid the notebook on Captain Peters' desk and walked out to his car. He should feel happy that they had more information to go on. He should. But he wasn't. Not at all.

33

Charly finished up her meeting with Falcon and Creed; they had a plan. She now stood at the supply cabinet handing out comm units, ammo, flack vests, and anything else they would need for tonight. They had a system to check out what they used. She had a belt she carried her implements on—they called them their utility belts, harkening back to the Batman show they watched together in the living room when they were chilling. Lately that happened less and less. Since the agency had hired them to replace Operation Live Again in finding missing kids and pedophiles, they'd had far too much work. It was a financial boon, but a sad reminder of what the world had become.

The door opened and Deacon walked in with Sam behind him.

"Hey Babe, your boyfriend is here." Deacon called across the room. Charly's chest, neck, and face heated. A few chuckles were heard around the room and Sam looked at her and winked.

Charly walked over to Sam but as she neared, the look on his face made her stomach twist. "What's wrong?"

"So, if you all want to see this, I'm hoping it will help in the short term to find Haylie, in the long term, others and the person or people who are paying money for these kids."

Sam walked over to the conference table and laid the sheets of paper on the table. He looked at Charly and said, "You may want to sit down."

He pulled up the sheet that had Olive and Haylie's names on it and laid it in front of her.

"We found notebooks in the tobacco store today. I'll tell you more about that in a while, but first, these appear to be the names of the girls and boys the Smiths had or have in their custody." He pointed to Olive's name. "Olive is here, six lines after Haylie. I believe Olive told you that they got Haylie first and then Olive had a fit and her mother sold her to the Smiths after. It looks like there are four kids in between them. The kids in between, three girls and one boy, all have dates after the price, indicating they've already been sold. From what I've been able to figure out, they keep the kids until they're twelve, then they sell them. I don't know why the age is important, but it seems to be the pattern."

Charly looked at the list and anger and disgust rose in her. Nausea roiled in her stomach but she took a deep slow breath as she looked at the papers. "What do the V and the N mean?"

Sam shook his head. "I'm not sure, but I think it must mean virgin or not. Eleese had a baby and she has an N.

She was also sold for much less. Based on the little bit I know about traffickers; virgins are a hot commodity. The amount of money they get for them appears to represent that."

Falcon Montgomery, who'd sat to Charly's right, slammed his fist on the table. "Disgusting fuckers."

Sam nodded and Charly gulped.

"Haylie will be twelve in a few weeks."

"Yes." Sam touched Charly's shoulder. "But we'll have her back before then. Tonight."

Charly nodded and tried catching her breath.

Creed had been silent until now. He was often quiet. He had been a SEAL and wore a prosthetic on his right leg, from the knee down. He was well-rounded by way of skills but he excelled at swimming and explosives.

"I say we go in now. Let's not risk them waiting till dark. The pressure is on and it can make them unpredictable. We go in now. If they're prepping to leave, we'll catch them off guard."

Falcon responded. "I agree."

Emmy came to sit across the table from Charly. "Charly, I agree. Go in now. There's a field behind the Paxton house, you can go in through the field which will provide some cover."

Emmy laid the satellite photograph of the house on the table and pointed at the field. "I've been in contact with the police department in Paxton, they'll provide some security for you by blocking off the road at either end so if the Smiths do try to leave, they'll be stopped. They're in place now."

Charly nodded. "Okay. I'm ready." She looked over at Sam. "Are you?"

Sam smiled at her and her heart felt light. "You bet. Let's go find Haylie."

Charly stood and tightened her utility belt. She then looked over at Sam. "You're going to need a comm unit. I presume you have a weapon?"

Sam patted his hip. "Never go anywhere without it."

Emmy stood. "Okay. Piper and Deacon on comm units and satellite surveillance. Falcon, Creed, and Charly, recon and recover. Sam, I assume you're with Charly."

Emmy smiled and so did Sam. "Yes ma'am."

Emmy nodded. "I'll have Diego and Van on standby. Let's roll."

Charly took Sam's hand and they walked to the supply cabinet. She located a comm unit and closed the door. "I'll help you put it on when we get close."

Sam nodded. "I'll drive. I have my weapons cache and extra ammo in my car. Plus, my radio if I need to call anything in."

Charly fell in behind Creed and Falcon as they walked out. The ride in the elevator up to the main floor and the garage was quiet, everyone mentally preparing for their mission. Charly sent up a silent prayer that Haylie would still be there. *Please, God, let her still be there.*

They all silently filed out of the elevator and to their respective vehicles. Sam reached over and took her hand. Her left hand. She looked down and once again she wished she could feel it. Feel him. He raised their joined hands and kissed her fingers; tears welled in her eyes at the sweet gesture. How did she get so lucky?

34

As he drove, he filled Charly in on the tobacco store and what had gone down. He also filled her in on Allan Rodinger and the bodies found in the field.

"I guess I should feel grateful that they keep the kids until they're twelve and don't rape them repeatedly. I guess it's a small consolation. But it still pisses me off that this is such big business and who the fuck is buying all these kids?"

"Rich men with many perversions is my guess." He responded.

Charly took a deep breath and let it out in a loud whoosh.

He reached over and took her hand in his. She smiled at their joined hands then looked over at him.

"What does it feel like to you?"

He looked at her briefly, then back to the road. "You mean your hand?"

"Yeah. When you take my left hand in yours, what does it feel like?"

He shrugged his shoulders. "It feels like part of you."

"But, it's cold and largely inanimate."

"You can move your fingers." He held their joined hands up between them. To prove his point, she moved her fingers to squeeze his hand.

"What does it feel like for you?"

She laughed, "I can't feel anything Sam."

"But I notice you always looking at our joined hands. You must feel something or you wouldn't keep looking at them."

She raised her right hand and settled it over her heart. "I feel it in here."

He looked at her again, "That's why I do it." Sam navigated a corner then completed his thought. "None of us is perfect, Charly. Not me, not you, not anyone at the station, and of course not anyone at RAPTOR."

She nodded and looked out the windshield. "Yeah."

Sam pulled his vehicle to the edge of the road, just across the field from the house in Paxton. Charly's phone rang and she looked at the readout. "It's Skye. I'll put her on speaker."

Sam nodded and smiled at her.

"Hi Skye."

"Hey Charly. So Olive looked at the floor plan and said the two bedrooms marked two and three is where she'd been. There are bunk beds in both of those rooms. She also said there's a small room in the basement. When kids first go to the house, they're kept in the basement until the Smiths know they won't try to run away."

"How do they know that?"

Skye sniffed on the other end of the phone and Sam felt queasy. "She said after she ate food sometimes she would sleep for a long time. Then Haylie told her not to eat too much because it was drugged."

"Wow." Charly's eyes were glassy from unshed tears. She swallowed and he came to the rescue.

"Skye, this is Sam Bowers. Thank you for asking Olive about the house. We're on our way out there now. Maybe don't say anything to Olive until we know if Haylie is there. Just in case."

"Hi Sam. Thank you."

Sam ended the call and let go of Charly's hand and reached up to her nape and squeezed her gently. She reached over with her left hand and laid it on his leg. It was a connection. He gave her a few minutes to compose herself, then cleared his throat. "Ready?"

"Yeah."

She pulled the comm unit out of the box and handed it to him. "Clip this inside your shirt or the waistband of your pants, put this part in your ear. When you need to talk you can tap this right here." She touched a little button on the earpiece. "When we go in, turn the unit to 'Open' here and you'll always be on so you don't have to have a free hand to talk to headquarters."

Sam clipped the comm unit onto his waistband and tucked the earpiece in his ear. Charly switched hers on and spoke to Piper and Deacon.

"Charly checking in."

"We can hear you Charly." Piper responded.

Sam turned his on 'Open' and repeated. "Sam Bowers checking in."

Deacon replied. "We've got you Sam. Welcome aboard."

Falcon and Creed each checked in and they were set to go.

Sam got out of his car and popped the trunk. He put his vest on, made sure he had additional ammo and checked his weapon. Charly walked to the edge of the field and waited for him. Once he was ready, he walked to Charly's side and she nodded.

"Sam and I are walking through the field now. Creed and Falcon, are you in place in the front?"

Creed answered. "In place. We're behind a grouping of bushes to the south side of the house. Once you're in place to clear the field, let us know. We'll go in."

"Roger." Charly responded.

Sam looked over at Charly and she smiled, then nodded. They stepped into the tall grasses, Sam had to crouch down a lot more than Charly did, but he was determined. They tried keeping their footprint as small as possible, avoiding undue notice from anyone who may be looking out of the house. It was a bonus for them that the field ran not only behind this house but the neighboring house as well, and the garage partially shielded them from view.

It didn't take them long to reach the edge of the field and Sam called it in. "We're at the edge of the field."

He looked over at Charly and she smiled and winked at him.

Creed and Falcon's heavy breathing could be heard over the comm units as they moved in place; Creed then called out their location.

"Front door right."

Falcon responded, "Front door left."

Sam looked over at Charly and nodded. Then crouch-walked to position on either side of the back door and once in place Charly reported. "Charly back door right."

"Sam back door left."

Sam pulled his weapon and so did Charly.

Creed counted, "Three. Two. One."

The loud crash of the front door being kicked in could be heard and a woman's voice was screaming.

Sam kicked in the back door and he entered gun first and cleared the kitchen. "Clear - kitchen."

Charly entered behind him. Together they listened as Falcon and Creed subdued the screaming woman, Creed yelling, "Are you Tammy Smith?"

"Who the fuck wants to know?"

"I do you piece of shit."

She let go a string of profanities before a loud slap was heard.

"Living room clear." Falcon called.

Sam stepped into the living room first, he could feel Charly behind him. He walked down the hall, the first bedroom was one that Olive had said she hadn't been in, but just in case he stuck his gun, then his head around the door, noted it was empty but still stepped inside and slid open the closet door to make sure they wouldn't be ambushed.

He shook his head to Charly and she proceeded to the bedroom marked two. She noted the door was locked—she raised her foot and kicked it several times before her foot went through the hollow door. She then continued to kick until she'd made a hole big enough to crawl through. Huddled in the corner was a young girl about ten or eleven years old. She had blond hair and big scared blue eyes. Her knees were tucked up to her chest and her arms wrapped around her knees.

"What's your name?"

"Aimee."

"Come with me Aimee, I'll get you home."

Sam let Charly work with Aimee and he went to the last bedroom. The door was locked so he kicked at it, breaking the lock on the first kick. Inside was another little girl, with dark hair and frightened dark eyes. She looked to be a little younger than the first girl, but it was hard to tell.

"What's your name?" Sam asked.

"Julie."

"Julie, I'm Sam and we're going to take you home. Can you walk?"

She nodded but moved slowly, likely not sure what to do. Sam waited for her to walk to him, and as she squeezed through the hole in the door he turned and saw Charly, jaw set and determined, walk away with Aimee.

Charly called on her comm unit, "Sam and I have two young girls. I haven't found Haylie yet. Creed and Falcon, we're coming out to the living room."

"Roger."

Julie softly said to Sam. "Haylie is in the basement. She was bad and Tammy got mad at her."

Charly turned and looked at Julie. "Where is the basement honey?"

Julie pointed to a door just off the kitchen and Charly nodded.

Charly preceded him to the stairs, but Sam was close behind her. Falcon took Aimee and Julie out to the road where police officers were to meet them and take the girls to the police station to be reunited with their families.

Falcon reported in. "Girls are safe."

Charly held her gun up and slowly walked along the edge of the stairs, Sam close behind her. As they neared the bottom two steps, Sam moved over to the other side of the stairwell, and peered around the edge of the wall. He shook his head and Charly stepped down one more step. She peered further around the wall, looked at him, and shook her head. She moved her gun to her left hand, which wouldn't shoot, but could hold it while she searched for a light fixture, but Sam touched her shoulder and shook his head. He motioned with his head for her to change places with him and normally she'd likely argue with him but it was to his advantage that she just wanted to get to Haylie.

Sam reached around and ran his hand slowly along the wall, finally finding a switch and turning the light on. He peered around the wall and then disappeared. Charly followed him into the basement and gasped when she saw what he was looking at. A little girl, about eleven years old, with dirty blond hair and blue eyes was sitting on a grimy little bed, her foot chained to the leg of the bed, which was bolted to the floor so she couldn't lift it and get out of her confinement. Sam began working to remove the chain, or the bolt, looking around the room for any tool to use.

Charly asked, "Are you Haylie?"

The girl looked into Charly's eyes then slowly nodded. Charly gasped then called into the comm unit, "We found her we..."

A loud thump sounded behind Sam and he turned to see a man standing over Charly with a pipe in his hand.

35

H er head throbbed. The jostling she felt right now didn't help at all. She tried opening them but the light stabbed at her eyes.

"Hang on, Charly." Sam's voice was gruff and he sounded scared.

She heard Falcon. "I've got Haylie."

Haylie. They'd found Haylie. Sam jostled them through a doorway. "She's coming around. Where's the ambulance?"

Ambulance? Haylie. "Sam. Haylie?"

"Falcon has Haylie, Charly. Just stay with me."

Oh, her head hurt so bad. Sirens could be heard getting closer. "Sam."

"Hang on Charly." He laid her down and she could feel the grass poking through her t-shirt at the back. She reached up to feel her head, it hurt so bad.

Sam's hands stopped her hand. "Don't touch it Charly. The ambulance will be here soon."

"What happened?"

"The Smiths were ready to make a sale today. Haylie. The buyer was in the basement with her when we came down. He hid in a backroom and hit you on the back of the head with a pipe."

"Oh my God. We were just in time."

"Yeah."

"Where is he? Did you get him? The buyer?"

"I punched his lights out, sent Haylie upstairs, and now I'm taking care of you."

The sirens stopped and people could be heard running toward her.

"I need you to step back sir. Tell me what you have here."

Sam's voice shook as he relayed her injury. "I put my shirt over the wound and added pressure to stop the bleeding. She was just talking."

"Ma'am. What's your name?"

"Charly." Her voice sounded foreign to her ears.

"Charly, what month is it?"

She swallowed. "September."

"Can you tell me if your vision is blurred?"

Charly opened her eyes and closed them quickly. The light was blinding.

"Too bright."

"Okay. I have to have a look, so bear with me."

His voice was nice, calm, and reassuring, but she wanted to hear Sam's voice. The EMT tried shielding her from the bright light and lifted an eyelid and shined a light into her right eye first then her left. He was quick and efficient and the pain was tolerable.

"Okay, we're lifting you onto a gurney."

She didn't dare look at him, she kept her eyes closed. "Sam."

"I'll be right behind the ambulance, Charly. I'll be with you at the hospital."

She lifted her right hand and gave him a thumbs up. Then, smiling slightly, lifted her left hand and gave him another thumbs up. He chuckled. "You're going to be just fine."

"Damn right," she whispered.

She felt the movement as they quickly pushed her to the ambulance and lifted her inside. The jostling was minimal and actually all she wanted to do was sleep at this point.

"Charly, I need you to wake up."

"Sleep."

"I'm sorry Charly, you can't sleep now. We need you awake."

Another person in the ambulance said, "We're going to roll you to your right side Charly, and check the wound at the back of your head."

She felt herself roll, then stinging at the back of her head as they sprayed something on her wound to clean it. She listened to the foreign sounds of beeping, the sirens, the jostling of the ambulance, and the voices of the two EMTs working on her. She drifted off to sleep a few times and they always gently woke her, much to her annoyance.

Charly sat in the emergency room, her bed slightly raised, an IV in her arm, wearing an ugly gown with some sort of small pattern on it, which hurt to focus on. There was light music playing from a speaker somewhere and voices could be heard as people raced back and forth outside her room.

The sliding glass door opened and the curtain pulled back to reveal the best sight ever. Sam. He wore a dark blue t-shirt, not the green shirt he'd worn earlier. His face was marred with worry, the creases in his forehead pronounced. His eyes sought hers instantly and he smiled.

"Hey. How are you feeling?"

"My headache is subsiding a bit. They gave me something. They wouldn't let me fall asleep but honestly all I want to do is sleep for like twelve hours."

He chuckled and pulled a chair, one of those uncomfortable plastic chairs with the metal legs, to her bed and sat close. He held her right hand in both of his hands and kissed her fingers.

"I was so fucking scared, babe."

His eyes filled with tears and her heart swelled at the emotion this man felt for her.

"Is Haylie safe?"

"Yes. Skye and Lincoln came to the police station to pick her up. Olive was so happy and those two little girls hugged each other so tight. It was beautiful to see. Olive brought Haylie's horse blanket with her and they wrapped themselves up together and sat in between Lincoln and Skye as they answered questions."

A tear slid down Charly's cheek. "I wish I could have seen that."

"I know babe. I made sure to tell Olive you were the one who found Haylie."

Charly looked into Sam's eyes. "You found her, too."

"It was your determination that found her Charly."

She closed her eyes but Sam's lips on hers was more than enough to keep her awake.

"I love you, Charlesia Sampson."

She opened her eyes, his face was so close to hers, his warm breath on her cheek, and she stared into his unusual yet perfect eyes. One blue and one green. So uniquely Sam.

"I love you too, Samuel Bowers."

His smile was beautiful. His face shone with the love he felt for her and she prayed hers showed him her love. She now knew what that meant when someone said, "I can see the love in his eyes when he looks at me."

"Can we come in?" Skye said from the door.

Sam sat back and Charly slowly sat up. "Yes. Please. Yes."

Skye stepped inside and Olive, Haylie, and Lincoln followed her in.

They were striking together. Haylie had changed clothes and it looked like she'd taken a shower or cleaned up. She looked the same but different.

"Hi." Charly held her arms open and Olive walked to the bedside and lay her head on Charly's chest as Charly held her close. "I'm so happy you're happy Olive. It's all I want for you."

Olive cried in her arms for a while. Haylie came to stand beside Olive, rubbing her back as she hugged Charly. Sam had moved back to allow the girls room, but he stood by watching. Her guardian. Her lover. Her love.

Haylie finally spoke over the tears. "Thank you for finding me."

"Oh honey, you are so welcome." Charly reached out her right arm and Haylie stepped close. She didn't lean over and hug Charly, but she did allow Charly to hold her hand.

Charly looked over at Lincoln and Skye. Lincoln had his arm around Skye's shoulder as they watched the girls with Charly. Lincoln nodded to her. "Are you feeling alright, Charly?"

"Yeah."

Charly looked at Skye and mouthed, "Thank you."

36

Sam pulled a beef roast from the oven and set it on top of the stove. He carefully pulled it from the roasting pan and laid it on a carving board. He transferred thick slices of meat to a platter and arranged the cooked carrots and potatoes alongside.

"Oh my God, it smells so good." Charly said as she entered the kitchen.

Sam turned and held his arms open as she walked into them. "So do you. How was your shower?"

"Wonderful. And, bonus, my head didn't bleed. I must be healing, thanks to you being my nurse this past week."

"I'm happy to do it."

He kissed her lips and enjoyed her body pressed to his. He was sorry for the reason she'd stayed here with him this week, but he was happy to have the time with her. They laid around during the day. Sam did his usual chores and laundry, adding Charly's clothes to his. He mowed his lawn, did some gardening. Did the grocery shopping and generally enjoyed taking care of Charly. They'd had three visits this week from Lincoln, Skye, and the girls and each time Haylie looked better and better. And Olive, well her face said it all. She was happy to have Haylie at her side and both girls enjoyed the horses and staying with Lincoln and Skye.

Charly had mentioned a couple of times that she worried Lincoln and Skye would be going crazy wanting to get the girls out of their space, but they never let on.

"Let's eat before it gets cold." He kissed the tip of her nose then turned to bring the roast to the table.

Charly sat in her usual place, the spot to his left, so she could hold his hand with her right hand. "I want to feel you, Sam."

That almost made him cry.

He waited for her to fill her plate then he filled his.

"What are we watching on television tonight?" she asked as they ate.

"I found a television series I'd like to start. We can stream it and binge it. It's about a Hollywood detective. I've heard it's amazing from Rory."

"Okay. Sounds great."

His doorbell rang after only a few bites. "Are you expecting anyone?" he asked Charly.

She shook her head as he got up quickly to answer the door.

Lincoln, Skye, Olive, and Haylie stood outside.

"Hi, come in."

They stepped inside as Charly walked into the living room. Olive immediately ran to her for a hug. Haylie was always a bit more reserved but she walked to Charly and hugged her briefly, then stepped back.

Charly went to Skye and hugged her. "Have you eaten?"

"We actually did. I'm so sorry, we're interrupting your dinner."

"Please don't worry. Sam's been feeding me like a horse this past week and if I eat much more, we'll be going shopping for larger clothes."

Charly laughed and he chuckled along with her, although Sam thought she looked perfect as she was.

Sam shook Lincoln's hand and closed the door.

"Please take a seat."

Skye's eyes scanned the room as she searched for any focal point besides Charly's gaze. Lincoln reached for her hand and settled Skye next to him on the sofa. The girls fell in, one on either side of the couple.

Charly put her arm around Sam's waist as he guided her toward the recliner and sat her on his lap.

Lincoln started. "We were excited to come and talk with you. We've been mulling this over. This week we've spoken with Hadleigh Keach and the girls, and, well..." He looked over at the girls, then Skye. "We'd like to adopt Olive and Haylie."

Silence. Everyone sat perfectly still. The term you could have heard a pin drop was absolutely one hundred percent true.

Finally, Charly leaned forward. He watched her swallow then she looked at Olive and Haylie. "Girls? Is this what you want? I promised Olive I'd only let you live somewhere that you'd be happy."

Olive looked at Haylie and both girls smiled. Then Olive said, "We want to. We like living there. We always get to eat. We have clean clothes. Skye bought us both comforters for our beds with horses on them. We got to pick out twin beds today. And we love Huckleberry and Blue. And Skye and Lincoln."

Sam rubbed Charly's back slowly as she sat back. "Haylie?"

"Yes. I'd like to live there. I never want to go back home. And Lincoln showed me the security. No one will ever take me again and he promised they will never sell us."

Charly gasped and raised her hands to her mouth. Skye spoke for the first time.

"I love having the girls at home with us. When Lincoln has to be away for work, they are wonderful to have and we keep each other company. We didn't want to start our own family because we're both in our mid-forties. Having a baby now would make us in our sixties when that baby graduated. We'd made a decision to not do that. But, these girls..." She looked at the girls and smiled. The love for them was in her eyes. "They belong with us. We all belong together."

Lincoln wrapped his arm around Skye's shoulders and squeezed her. "We'd always want you to come and visit whenever you want. Anytime."

Charly looked back at Sam, her eyes searching his, for what? Acceptance? His thoughts?

He smiled at her; his hand reached up and cupped the back of her head, tenderly so as not to hurt her injury. "It seems perfect doesn't it?"

Tears ran in streams down her cheeks. "It does."

Charly turned and looked at them all. She swallowed and he knew she was struggling to talk, so he rubbed her back and let her know he was there for her.

Finally, she smiled at them. "I'm so happy for all of you."

Olive walked over to them and wrapped Charly in a hug. "I love you, Charly."

Charly burst out crying as she held Olive and Sam felt about as useful as a log. He never knew what to do when women cried.

37

Charly tucked the last bowl of food into the refrigerator and closed the door. Sam closed the dishwasher door and started the cleaning cycle. He turned to look at her and she melted. Not really, but oh, he made her feel all the feelings.

He smiled at her as he approached. It was 'that' smile.

"How are you feeling?"

Charly giggled. "Good. How are you feeling?"

"Good. Really good."

He kissed her and she kissed him right back. He wasted no time bending his knees and lifting her so her feet were off the floor. Her legs wrapped around him as her lips continued to dance with his. Their kisses started out slow, wet, and dreamy. But soon his breathing was choppy, his hands roamed over her body, especially her ass, pulling her tighter to his body.

He pulled away just an inch, "I have a confession."

Charly looked into his eyes, now a bit wary. "Okaaay."

"I don't want to watch television."

Charly laughed. "Oh, what did you want to do then?"

A slow lazy smile spread across his handsome face. "I want to make love to you."

"That sounds like the best idea ever. But after ten minutes, what will we do?"

His brows furrowed for a minute and she couldn't help it, she burst out laughing. "I'll show you ten minutes, Charlesia."

"Oh, now I'm Charlesia? Well, Samuel, let's see what you've got."

He almost growled as he walked them back to the bedroom. "If you weren't healing from an injury, I'd toss you over my shoulder."

"Well, let's just say I can't wait to be healed."

He slapped her ass, the loud crack startling her, then she squealed.

He lay her gently on the bed, and she started undoing her jeans, tugging her shirt off then her undergarments as she watched him do the same. He was strong, large—imposing would be a good descriptor—but he had a ready smile when they were together and she enjoyed watching all his moods. Especially this one. This was the best Sam right here.

As he dropped his drawers she smiled, he was firm and erect and ready. Yep, the best Sam right here. Well, one of them. All his moods were pretty great. She absently licked her lips as she looked at his cock, all of it, and he growled. "You're a beautiful woman Charly."

She smiled at him, "You make me feel beautiful."

"Good."

He lifted her legs and pulled her to the edge of the bed, then dropped to his knees. Before she could lift herself up on her elbows, his warm mouth was on her. His tongue slowly swiped a circle around her clit before his lips sucked her in, then let go. Her head dropped back onto the bed and she mumbled. "Holy hell."

He repeated that motion as he worked a finger into her, in and out until she felt fully penetrated. Slowly he moved his finger inside her, crooking it up slightly as he pulled out then pushed back in. Her legs shook at the overwhelming and exciting sensations. His mouth continued laving her, alternating between circling her clit and licking her, then sucking her in. The changing motions consumed her.

He sucked her in again and added pressure as his finger slipped in and out of her and before she could comprehend what had just happened, her orgasm rolled over her like a fire over dried wood. Even her vision went slightly black.

He pulled his finger out of her, his lips kissed up her body, suckling each breast in turn before his arm slid under her shoulders and pulled her body up further on the bed.

He nestled himself between her legs, his eyes captured hers, "I love you, Charly."

She smiled, "I love you too, Sam."

He positioned himself at her entrance then froze. He pulled away and twisted his body but she grabbed his hands with hers. "Don't. It doesn't matter to me."

"You sure?"

"Yeah."

He didn't hesitate. He turned back to her, positioned himself at her entrance and slowly pushed himself inside. Oh the feeling of Sam filling her would never get old.

"My God Charly. Unfuckingbelievable." He huffed out.

She raised her legs and wrapped them around his hips, their bodies now fully joined, both of them connected in a way that only lovers connect. Not just physically but emotionally too. She'd fallen in love with Sam long ago. Mostly it was the idea of him. But now she knew Sam, the man. She loved him. Sam the lover was incredible.

He continued to set their pace, slow long strokes in and out, each one felt better than the last, each one new and exciting. His body hovered over hers, his lips kissed her ear, her head, her forehead. Each thrust of his hips brought her closer to a new high.

He changed up their dance, by pushing inside then thrusting his hips forward to add pressure where she needed it. Their skin was heated and flushed. A fine sheen of sweat had formed on each of them, their bodies working in unison to pleasure the other. Her arms wrapped around him, pulling him tighter as she climbed that hill she so badly wanted to fall over, the crest almost there. Each thrust brought her closer until finally her body shook, she moaned out his name as her orgasm rose and fell.

Sam followed her over that hill, pushing in once more and holding still as he spilled into her. His groan in her ear telling her she'd given him pleasure and that was the best part of making love. Sure, you received pleasure, but giving pleasure to someone you loved, that was sensational.

"Oh my God Charly." He panted. His lips kissed the shell of her ear, his breathing coming in rapid bursts. "Oh my God."

Her right hand slid into the hair at his nape and held his head close. "Yeah."

38

Monday morning Sam walked into the police station, his vacation, such as it was, over. Charly had gone back to RAPTOR, too, though she planned on coming back to his place tonight. He told her to pack a suitcase and bring it over. She laughed and he was now sorry he didn't get more of a commitment. He should ask her to move in, that's what he wanted. At this time in his life, in his later thirties, he knew cream of the crop when he saw it. Charly was grade A prime. He believed she felt the same way, but they hadn't had the conversation.

Rory Richards tapped on the door frame of his office. "Sam, have you gone in and interviewed Maddox yet?"

"Nope, I'm going in after I speak with Phillip. What've you learned from him since I've been gone?"

Rory sat in the chair across from Sam's desk. "Not a damned thing. He's locked up tighter than Fort Knox."

Sam sat back and studied Rory. "Do we know anything yet?"

"Only that he's from Las Vegas. He won't say where he works but in doing a search of his social media, it looks like he's somehow associated with the Las Vegas Sinners football franchise. The majority of his pictures are him with the team members and some of the coaching staff."

Sam leaned forward; his brows bunched. "You think the team or someone from the team is involved in trafficking?"

Rory shrugged. "Or just him. He has big money connections. I've been doing some reading on trafficking. Do you know Superbowl weekend every year is the time most trafficking happens? Big-dollar high rollers come skating into town, whatever town it is. They drink. They're horny. They want to walk on the wild side. They pay big money for kids, especially virgins, and use them to satiate their sexual proclivities. It's disgusting."

"Fuck that's gross."

"Right. So either this asshole is involved in something like that or he's working for someone on the team. Or, maybe the team isn't involved at all."

"I take it you saved the pictures you pulled down?"

"Yeah. They're in the file."

Sam nodded and patted the file on his desk. "What about Phillip Smith? Did you get anything out of him?"

"Nope. He only wants to talk to you."

"Nice. What about his mom?"

Rory sat forward and grinned. "She's acting all tough but I think we can work her. She's a greedy bitch and she only thinks of herself so when you go in there, you'll need to come up with something that will make her think she's getting something Phillip and Howie aren't."

Sam nodded. "Okay. Where are you off too?"

"I'm going to the hospital to see if I can get Howie to talk. He's being weaned off his meds now that they've taken the bullet out."

"Perfect."

Rory stood at the same time Sam did. "Charly doing okay?"

"Yeah, she went back to work today. She had a horrendous headache for about three days but that's subsided. She goes back to the doctor tomorrow for a scan and a check."

Rory smiled and nodded. "Glad to hear it."

Rory left his office and Sam grabbed the file, a note pad, pen, and his coffee cup. He took a deep breath and headed to the interrogation room to speak with Phillip first. He'd told the booking sergeant first thing this morning, that he wanted to interrogate Phillip right away and Jerard after. He needed to gather as much information on Jerard as possible because after what he'd done to Charly, Sam wanted to kill him. Letting him walk was not an option, he hoped.

He walked into the interrogation room and there sat Phillip Smith. Slouched over, a frown on his face and attitude front and center.

"Phillip, you don't look happy to be here."

Phillip's eyes wandered up to Sam's then quickly back to the table.

"Nothing to say? I figured by now you'd be excited to talk to me."

Phillip looked up at him again. "Why would you think that?"

Sam sat at the table and lay his forearms in front of him on top of the file.

"Well, by now Maddox has been chatting away and your mother, who cares more about herself than any one of you, is cutting deals left and right. She'll be out of here this afternoon."

"You're so full of shit Bowers."

Sam chuckled. "Am I?"

He opened the file and pulled out a picture of Jerard Maddox with one of the team members from the Las Vegas Sinners.

"You see, Maddox has big money. Connections. And backing for his little child trafficking ring. So he doesn't give two shits about you Smiths. There are dozens of Smiths in the world of Jerard Maddox. Word has it his lawyer will be here later today. Been denied bail last week because he's a flight risk, but thinks if he turns you Smiths in, it'll help his case. Your mamma doesn't like the sound of that, so she's singing."

"Look. All I want is Eleese and Shiloh."

Sam kept his face neutral, at least he hoped he did. "Why do you want Eleese back?"

"She's mine. She loves me and I love her."

"How old is Eleese?"

Sam pretended to look at sheets in the file to keep him looking official and disinterested.

"Fourteen."

"So, you're in love with a fourteen-year-old? How old are you, Phillip?"

"Why does that matter? It doesn't matter." His voice rose, close to yelling.

"Well, according to the law it matters. Is Shiloh the baby?"

Phillip turned his head and looked at the wall. Sam continued.

"Is Shiloh your baby? Is she a Smith?"

He saw Phillip swallow but his posture didn't change.

"Look, Phillip, we'd like to bring Eleese and Shiloh home, too. Are you saying she's in Las Vegas? Do you know what they do to young girls in Las Vegas?"

"He said she'd just be a maid."

Sam laughed. Phillip was really stupid to believe that. Where there's money to be made it would be made. No matter who they used to make it.

Phillip's voice lowered. "He promised."

"You think he kept that promise?"

"Why don't you ask him?"

"I intend to. Why did you sell Eleese if you wanted to keep her?"

Phillip scratched his head and sniffed. "I didn't. Tammy did when I wasn't there."

"So she did it behind your back?" Sam shifted more papers in the file. "Told you she didn't care about anyone else. She sold her own granddaughter."

Phillip glared at him, his jaw tightened and he rotated his shoulders.

Sam sat back and took a breath. "Tell you what. Give me something to hold Jerard Maddox for a while longer, then I'll see if we can find out where Eleese and Shiloh are."

Phillip swallowed and didn't say anything, so Sam sat back and waited. His heart raced; they were close. He kept his eyes glued to Phillip and didn't look away. Someone this weak would cave shortly. At least, that was Sam's hope.

"Tammy sold her because she was mad at me for ruining her. Said I cost them a lot of money. But I love her. She was nice to me."

"Did your mom sell her to Maddox?"

"Yes." Phillip swallowed hard; tears formed in his eyes.

"How much?"

Phillip hesitated and swallowed again and finally closed his eyes and said, "$25,000."

39

Charly ended her call with Sam and walked over to the computers where Piper and Deacon were working.

"So Sam just said Jerard Maddox is involved with the Las Vegas Sinners. He's the jerk who bought Eleese and he was here to buy Haylie."

She absently rubbed the back of her head.

"Can you guys run a full scope on Maddox and see what his affiliation is with the Sinners? Then find any known business associates or activities. Maybe he's running a side hustle, either on his own or for someone else."

Piper's mouth dropped open. "Didn't that team just move to Las Vegas? They were from California or something, right?"

Charly smiled at Piper. "Pipes, I didn't know you followed football."

Piper shrugged. "I like the tight pants and the moves." She motioned with her hands in an hour-glass figure, with her shrapnel laced back, she couldn't or wouldn't do that in fear she'd end up paralyzed.

Deacon laughed. "You two. What are we going to do with you? This one here..." He pointed to Charly, "Is all gaga over Sam Bowers, a lowly detective. And Pipes, you watch football for the tight pants?"

"What do you like Deac?" Piper shot back.

"I like smart girls who like smart guys."

Charly looked at Piper and shrugged. "Sam's smart. I'm smart. Piper's smart. Emmy's smart. Who's not smart here, Deac?"

"I didn't say that. I...never mind. I'll run your full scan."

Deacon turned to his computer and Piper laughed at him, then said, "I'll help him. If I can keep my mind off of tight football pants that is."

Piper returned to her work and Charly giggled as she headed out to the police station. Sam said he'd share files with her. But first, she was going up to pack up a couple days of clothing.

On the first floor, Charly swung through the kitchen to see what Sheldon had cooking for lunch. She stopped and pulled a bottle of water from their liquids' refrigerator. They had three large refrigerators in the kitchen; they spanned a full wall. One was all food supplies. One was filled with water, electrolyte-supplement waters such as Gatorade or other brands, and the third was leftovers, condiments, etc.

Sheldon turned as she closed the door. "Hey Charly, haven't seen you in a while. How are you feeling?"

"Better now. Thank you."

"Why don't you bring that big fella of yours here for dinner sometime so we can all decide if he's worthy of you?" His smile was genuine, but his tone was clipped.

"I will. What about tomorrow night?"

"Perfect. I'll make extra food."

He grinned but she knew he was only half kidding. Sheldon liked showing off his skills a bit and a new face in the dining room would be a chance for him to do that.

Charly quickly packed, then dropped her suitcase to the floor and wheeled it out of her door and to the garage.

As she started to back out of the garage her phone rang. She tapped the Bluetooth button on her steering wheel, "Charly."

"Hey babe. On your way?"

She smiled and her cheeks warmed. "Yeah."

"Did you pack a suitcase?"

"Yeah."

"Nice."

She giggled.

"So, I got permission from Captain Peters to let you sit in when I interrogate Tammy Smith. You want in?"

"Yes. Absolutely."

"Perfect. Come to my office first and I'll go over what we have already then we'll talk to her."

"Thanks Sam."

He was quiet for a minute then said, "Will you move in with me?"

"For real?"

"For real."

"I don't cook."

"I do."

"I'm not super domestic."

"We both make good money. Why don't we hire a house-keeper to come in once a week and clean the house? We can order meals, either those kits, or we can learn to cook other things together. Or, we'll figure it out. Basically, anything can be worked out. I'd like to be with you all the time. I want to wake up every morning with you and go to bed every night with you."

She swallowed because in all her life, especially after losing her arm, she never dreamed she'd find that guy. That one she wanted to spend all her free time with.

"What about..."

He sighed on the other end of the line and she even liked that. "What babe?"

"Protection. If we don't use it, there'll be kids."

"Is that bad?"

Goose bumps formed on her arms and her nipples pebbled thinking about having Sam's child. It would likely be huge.

"Well, we're new, Sam. I mean, I want to be with you for certain. No questions. But..."

"Babe, are you worried about my commitment?"

Charly navigated a turn and sighed. "A girl has to be sure Sam. All of a sudden one day a newer hotter woman walks in the police station door and you're gone and I'm stuck with a bunch of kids by myself."

Sam laughed on the other end of the line. "Now we're having a bunch of kids and I'm having an affair? Holy shit, Charly."

She didn't say anything because it sounded stupid and needy even to her own ears.

Sam sighed. "Look babe. Come to the station and we'll interrogate Tammy. Then, we'll have a chat. Deal?"

"Deal."

He chuckled as he ended the call.

Charly felt sheepish for going...there. She rolled her head around to relieve the tension then let out a long breath. She turned into the lot at the Lynyrd Station PD and parked her car. Clearing her throat and allowing herself to settle, she climbed out and walked into the station.

The officer behind the front desk looked up at her and smiled. "Sam's waiting for you Charly." He pointed behind him, "Second door on the left."

"How did..." She smiled. "Thank you." By now the word was out and she'd met enough of the officers here over the past couple of weeks that they all knew what she looked like.

She walked through a door to her left and the officer buzzed her in. She then walked in the direction the officer had pointed and noted which door was Sam's. Just before she got to Sam's door, Eydie Evans walked out of Sam's office.

"Hi Charly. How're you feeling?" She greeted.

"Hi Eydie. I'm good as new. I had a good nurse though." She smiled at the officer and received a genuine smile in return.

Eydie walked on and Charly stepped into Sam's office. He made the room seem overly small. But he always looked scrumptious.

"Hey handsome."

"Hey babe. You look as beautiful as ever."

His smile was genuine and she allowed happiness and love to wrap itself around her for a moment.

Sam stood and motioned for them to walk out of the room. As he came around his desk, his hand lay at the small of her back and ooh, those feelings.

In the conference room next to his office, he laid a thick file on the table and pulled a chair out for her to sit. He took the seat next to hers and lowered his voice.

"So, first, I want you to know a couple of things." He leaned over and pushed the door closed, though the glass surrounding the room still kept them visible to everyone gawking as they walked by outside; clearly he wanted some privacy. "Charly. I love you. Not only do I love you, but I've never felt this way about anyone ever in my life. Keep in mind I was married before. It didn't end because either of us cheated. We were young, ambitious and we quickly grew apart once we both matured and figured out what we wanted to do with our lives. I wanted to be a detective. That means long irregular hours. She wanted to be a nine-to-fiver. For her, she needed regular hours and a set pattern to be happy. She has that now with her new husband."

His hand rested on top of her right hand. "I can't give you regular hours. I can't even say my job isn't dangerous. Neither can you. But I can give you my whole heart and a promise that I will always be here for you and with you. As we decide how we want to move forward, I want you to know it's serious for me. I even called my parents this morning and told them about you."

"You did?"

He nodded and smiled at her. "I did. They want to know when they can meet you."

She giggled. "I'd like to meet them too."

Sam's smile, it was...magic to her soul. "So, are we good and can we get down to business?"

She giggled. "Yes."

He opened the file and showed her the information they'd gathered.

"Phillip confirmed that Tammy's the one who sold Eleese. He also confirmed that Jerard Maddox is the person who bought her, and that Eleese's baby, Shiloh, is his. Olive confirmed that her mom first sold Haylie to Tammy, then herself, and she saw her mom take the money. We've got Tammy dead to rights in prison for child trafficking. We remind her of that. As far as we're concerned, the Smiths are finished. We're still going through information on them and my department will continue following the leads on the arms-distribution channels to see if we can move up the chain and get those at the top. Your department will need to continue following Maddox's trail to bring that chain down. So when we go in, we need to focus on getting everything we can on Maddox from Tammy while making her think we're willing to cut a deal to keep her out of prison without actually telling her that we will."

Charly looked at the pictures of Maddox and his football cohorts and nodded.

"Piper and Deacon are running as much information as they can on Maddox now."

"Good. Are you ready?"

"Yep."

He nodded then stood. "Let's go get her."

40

S am spent the following week trailing down the gunrunners, dealers, and scumbags associated with the Smiths. Howie Smith had given them some information, but he was reluctant to give too much. That was, until Sam told him everything Tammy had shared. Then Howie got mad. Once he realized Tammy was all about saving her own skin and no one else, Howie started sharing all kinds of information with them and Sam had a busy damned week. But it was worth it when he came home at night to Charly. One night he didn't get home until after she'd gone to bed. But crawling in beside her and wrapping her up in his arms felt so right.

Two nights he came home only to find she'd gone to the RAPTOR compound and sweet-talked Sheldon into packing them up some food to go. She arranged it on plates and had it ready when he walked in. But she quickly admitted she didn't make it.

The other nights, they both got home late, ate something not-so-healthy, and went to bed exhausted. But, he'd never felt more alive.

Now he had work to do. A plethora of phone calls to make, arrangements to be made, and things to get done.

He called Rory Richards first. Then Eydie Evans. He called a convenience store manager on the other side of town. The hospital ER doctor and two of the nurses. Now he had to call Emmy Copeland and talk to her. This needed to be pulled off without a hitch and everyone had to do their part to make it happen. It was just that important.

By the end of the day Sam was wiped completely out. He got home before Charly and put a chicken in the oven, but proceeded to fall asleep on the couch. Charly walked in the front door and yelled, "Sam, fire. Get up, the place is on fire!"

Sam jolted awake and looked around, the living room was filled with smoke. "Open the windows, Charly. I'll pull dinner out of the oven."

He ran to the kitchen, mostly feeling his way around the room, until he got to the oven. Shoving his hands in oven mitts, he pulled open the oven door and jumped back as the dark smoke from inside billowed out in large puffs of dark clouds. He fanned the mitts before him, hoping to get enough of a view to see where the damned pan was and pull it out of the oven.

Seeing his opportunity, he pulled it out and dropped it on the stove top, slammed the oven closed and turned it off. He leaned over the kitchen sink and pushed the window open, then ran around the kitchen area opening windows.

Charly's coughs from the other room caught his attention and he went in search of her. "Charly?"

"I'm in the bedroom."

He felt his way down the hall as he heard Charly opening windows and coughing. It wasn't quite as bad at the back of the house. Sam found Charly and wrapped his arm around her, "Let's go sit outside for a bit while the house clears out."

He walked with her wrapped in his arms, down the hall and to the back door. As they stepped out onto the patio, Sam pulled two lawn chairs open and set them alongside each other. They both sat and gulped in large quantities of fresh air.

"Are you alright Charly?"

She laughed. "I'm fine. How about you?"

Sam coughed but nodded. "Good." He managed between coughs.

"Sounds like you're good." She smiled at him and his cheeks burned.

"I'll be fine." He took a few more gulps of air then quietly said, "I'm sorry about supper."

Charly burst out laughing. "Sam, I can cook like that. Why didn't you tell me you like your food well-done?"

He laughed despite his embarrassment. "I've never done that before. I'm just exhausted from this past week."

Charly scooted her chair closer to his and took his hand. "You've been working hard this week. Don't run yourself into the ground, mister."

"I won't." He chuckled.

She pulled her phone out and tapped a few times. He watched her as she listened then said, "I'd like a pizza delivered please."

Sam went inside and while the smoke still hung a bit heavy in the house, it was beginning to fade. Though he'd likely have to wash everything inside to get rid of the smell. He'd have the carpets cleaned tomorrow. He took two beers out of the refrigerator and twisted the tops off, tossing them in the garbage. He walked back outside and gave one to Charly and tapped the neck of his bottle to hers.

"Here's to pizza."

"Cheers."

His phone buzzed and he pulled it from his pocket and read the text. He re-read it to make sure he understood what it said. He swallowed and turned to see Charly looking at him, her forehead marred with worry.

"Sam, what?"

He took a deep breath. "I've been offered a job."

He watched her swallow but she said nothing. Her jaw clenched and he knew she was holding back emotion.

"What kind of job?"

"Sheriff."

"Sheriff? But that's an elected position."

"Right. So, the Boones County Sheriff is retiring. No one has stepped up to run and if someone does, both the current Sheriff and the Mayor have agreed to back me in the election."

"Boones County." Charly swallowed. "That's here."

Sam smiled. "It is. It's actually perfect, isn't it? I get my promotion of sorts with the responsibility I've wanted, we stay here. We're together."

41

Charly woke and stretched. Sam was gone, his side of the bed sadly empty. She reached over and pulled his pillow to her and breathed in his scent. She loved his scent.

Lying on his pillow, she closed her eyes once again and allowed herself to fall back to sleep.

A ringing phone woke her from a blissful dream and she was instantly annoyed.

Charly snatched her phone from the bedside table. "Yeah."

His deep low chuckle gave her goose bumps. "Hey Babe."

She lay back in bed, and smiled. "Good morning. How long have you been gone?"

"A couple of hours. I had to oversee the transfer of Howie and Tammy Smith to their respective temporary prisons until their trials. Everyone is happy they're gone now.

Apparently all Tammy did was bitch for the past few weeks."

"Oh, good riddance. Are you coming home now?"

"In a little while, I still have some things to do."

"Okay. I'll see you later then. Love you Sam."

He chuckled. "Love you too Charly."

Just as she hung up, someone knocked on the front door. She took a deep breath and scrambled out of bed. The knock came again and she walked faster to get to the door. Peering through the peephole, she saw Piper standing outside.

Charly unlocked the door and opened it, "Hey Pipes, what's up?"

"I came to see if you want to go shopping with me. I'm going to Vegas to help Caiden and Creed investigate the Sinners. I think I'll need some help with my wardrobe to fit in out there."

"Come in." Charly walked toward the kitchen. "Coffee?"

"Yes."

"Okay." Charly pulled cups from the cupboard, then poured two cups from the pot Sam left on for her. Piper walked into the kitchen and smiled at her.

"You've been domesticated."

"No, I haven't."

"You have and it looks good on you."

Charly grinned and gently pushed Piper's cup toward her. She pointed to the creamer and sugar bowl, "Fixings are there, help yourself while I go shower and get ready."

"Take your time. Wear something sexy."

Charly stopped and turned to look at Piper. "Why?"

"Cause afterward I thought we'd go to lunch."

"Why would I dress sexy for lunch?"

"Well, I need to practice wearing sexy clothes and eating in a nice restaurant and figured you'd help me practice." She held her arms out and for the first time Charly noticed Piper's black dress and red heels.

"You look fantastic. Why do you have to practice all of that?"

Piper leaned against the counter and crossed her arms. "Charly, all I wear at work is t-shirts, jeans, and boots or slip-on shoes. I never, well rarely, leave the building. My God we work there, we eat there, and I live there. I feel like I've let myself go with my social skills. My new favorite phrase is "for fuck's sake" and if it wasn't for you and Emmy and to some extent Shelby and Hadleigh running around the building I'd have no graceful skills at all. You all make me at least want to be feminine. I'm feeling like one of the guys."

Charly laughed out loud and walked to Piper. Wrapping her right arm around Piper, 'cause she still didn't have her left arm on, she hugged her friend. "I felt like that for a while too. I've more of a mind to say you should ask Sophie Vickers or Roxanne Delany from over at the

GHOST house how to be sexy. I'm just a blue-jeans and sweater or shirt sort of girl."

"Well, they are very feminine and beautiful. But I know you better."

"Okay." Charly took a deep breath and picked up her coffee cup. "I'll be out in a bit. Wearing something sexy."

An hour later, they were in Piper's car and driving across town. Charly looked out the window. "Where are we going? There aren't any clothing stores over here."

"No, there aren't, but I wanted to make a stop first. Then we'll be on our way."

"You're acting weird Pipes. Are you sure you should be going on a mission?"

Piper giggled. "I'm absolutely sure. And you promised to be on the comm units helping me out."

"I'll be here. I want those assholes stopped."

Piper pulled into a convenience store parking lot and parked.

"Why do you have to run an errand here?"

"Just come in, you'll see."

"Dressed like this?"

"You look gorgeous."

Charly's brows furrowed. "That's what I mean. This place is gross. They never clean it and it smells inside."

"Come on Charly. Do me this favor please."

Piper quickly got out of her car and Charly was beginning to feel irritated with her. But when Piper stood in front of the car with her hands on her hips, Charly rolled her eyes and got out. Her short black dress was her big splurge last year that she'd made for a friend's wedding. The sparkly heels that went with it and matching clutch made her feel sexy.

She met Piper in front of the door and her friend smiled at her. "You do look gorgeous if I didn't say that earlier."

"Thanks Pipes."

Charly followed her friend inside the convenience store and down an aisle. At the end of the aisle, Piper turned and handed her a card. "Read this."

Charly's brows furrowed again. "What in the hell is..."

"Just read and stop asking so fucking many questions."

Charly took a deep breath, then opened the card. It was a picture of a soft white kitten on the front. On the inside, in handwriting she knew so well now, it said, "We first met here. I was investigating a shooting and you walked in. I thought you were the most beautiful woman in the world. Stunning. I remember having a hard time concentrating while you were here. Then, before I could find my tongue, you were gone. Sam."

"Wow." She looked at his handwriting and her heart thumped in her chest. Then she looked up and around the store. "Where is he?"

"He's not here."

A man in a black suit walked up to them then, and bowed slightly at the waist.

"Ms. Charlesia Sampson, my name is Charles. I'm to take you and your friend, Ms. Dillion, to your next stop."

"What?"

Piper tucked her arm through Charly's left arm and led her along the aisle and out to a gorgeous limousine sitting in the parking lot.

"But, what about your car Pipes?"

Caiden Marx, stepped out of the back of the Limo, "I'll take your car back Pipes."

"Caiden, what are you doing here? What in the hell is going on?"

Piper laughed and led Charly to the door of the limo Charles held open for them.

"Sam has a surprise for you."

They climbed in the limo and Charles asked, "Would you ladies like champagne?"

Piper giggled. "Yes, please."

Charly sat in stunned silence as Charles opened a bottle of champagne and pulled two champagne flutes from the holder inside the car. He poured the first glass and handed it to her, which she quietly took with a bemused smile. Charles then poured another for Piper, placed the bottle in a holder, and closed the door.

He quietly got behind the wheel and as Piper lifted her glass to Charly, the limo took off from the parking lot. It took Charly a while to get her mind around what was going on. She held Sam's card in her left hand and looked down at it as it lay in her lap.

"What's this surprise for?"

Piper shrugged. "I don't know. He called a couple of weeks ago and gave me simple instructions. I'm following them. Now, I'll ask you not to badger me with questions, let's enjoy being pampered a bit."

Piper crossed her long slender legs, her red heels striking in the limo, Charly took a deep breath and then a sip of her champagne.

The limo pulled to a stop and Charly looked out the window.

"Hey, this is Harry Smith's house."

The back door opened and Charles held his hand out to assist her from the limo. She swallowed hard, her heartbeat once again increasing. She wasn't sure how she felt about this surprise. Piper stepped on the sidewalk alongside her and took her hand. "Come on."

Piper led her to the house and pulled a key from inside her clutch. They entered the house, which looked very much the same as it had the last time she'd been here. There was a large "X" on the floor, at the foot of the steps in blue painter's tape. On top of the "X" was another card. Piper nodded at her and Charly bent and picked up the card.

Her fingers shook as she opened it. This time it had the drawing of a girl with blonde curly hair sitting on a wooden fence, looking across a yard at a playing puppy.

She opened it and Sam's beautiful handwriting said, "I kissed you here for the first time. Not the most romantic place for a first kiss, but I just knew I couldn't let you walk out the door without kissing you. Not again."

Charly's eyes filled with tears as his writing wavered before her. She looked up at Piper and took a deep breath, "Is he here?"

"Nope. We've got another stop."

"If this weren't all so romantic, I'd think he was breaking up with me."

Piper laughed. "Yeah, I don't think that's it."

They returned to the limo where Charles stood dutifully by and repeated the motions from their last stop. Except for the opening of the champagne. This time Charles produced a small platter of cheese and crackers, refilled their champagne flutes and slipped out of sight.

She nibbled on the cheese and crackers and drank her champagne as Piper chatted about her exciting trip to Las Vegas, and the plans they were hatching to make contact with some of the team members to get inside.

"So, we're trying to locate the nightclubs they hang out at and we'll try and meet up with them there. That's one reason I wanted to go shopping. I do not have Vegas night-club clothes."

Charly heard Piper but her words were floating in the air somewhere. She tried remembering if this was some special day in their life. Sam's birthday wasn't until November. Hers was in April. They'd been dating around a month. She tried remembering the first day they started dating and smiled. They didn't really have a first date. Not like most people do.

The limo turned a corner and Charly looked out the window. They were at the hospital. She searched her brain for what they'd done here.

The door opened and Charles once again helped her out of the limo and Piper led her inside. When they entered the emergency room, which was a circular area with glass doors separating the exam rooms from the nurses' station, there stood a group of nurses, all in their scrubs, a bouquet of balloons on a counter and a card.

Charly swallowed the emotion that already welled up inside of her and Piper led her to the balloons. The nurses all had big smiles on their faces but said nothing. Her fingers were shaking so badly she could hardly open the card. When she did, a colored pencil drawing of a little house was on the front and inside, Sam's written note.

"I first told you I loved you here. You told me you loved me too. Charly, I'll never be able to tell you in words what saying that and hearing it back meant to me. I love you Charlesia Sampson. I love you."

The tears rolled down her face. A nurse handed her a tissue and smiled at her. "You're a very lucky woman."

Charly nodded and allowed herself to be pulled back to the limo in a daze so heavy she was beginning to have a hard time breathing.

She said little and Piper allowed her to sit in her silence and contemplate the things that had led up to this day.

The limo pulled to a stop and Piper giggled, "This is our last stop Charly. I love you too, you know."

Charly looked over at Piper, a big beautiful smile on her face. "I love you too, Pipes. Whatever all of this is, thank you for helping Sam with it. And me."

Piper leaned forward and hugged her. The door opened and there they stood outside of Sam's house. Her home now. She looked at Piper, her brows furrowed. "I thought we were going shopping."

Piper shrugged. "Maybe later?"

Piper walked with her to the front door and opened it. She stepped back and nodded to Charly.

When she walked in, she had a hard time catching her breath. Roses, beautiful roses, all of them orange, her favorite, stood in vases on the fireplace, on the floor, on the coffee table on the side tables, everywhere.

She looked around at the flowers and Sam walked out of the kitchen and into the living room. He looked so incredibly handsome dressed in a suit. He smiled and held his arms open to her. Her knees were weak but she walked to him and wrapped her arms around his waist and enjoyed the strength she felt as they stood together. Finally able to catch her breath, she stepped back.

"You've blown me away today, Sam."

He smiled; his voice was quiet. "This is the first place I made love with you. In our home, we made love, body, mind, and soul. I felt it, did you?"

She nodded. "I did."

He smiled again and bent down on one knee. "I love you Charly like I've never loved anyone. So completely it's scary. So fully I don't even feel like a whole person without you. Will you marry me?"

Marry him? Wow. She looked into his eyes, so uniquely Sam's, she couldn't even tell you which one she liked best, the blue or the green. His broad shoulders were drool-worthy, his body, well, dang, he was the whole package. But his heart? That was the most precious part of him and the thing she'd take care of the most.

"Yes, Sam. I'll marry you. I'll join with you to make you whole because then I'm whole too."

Sam pulled a black velvet box from his front pocket and opened it to show a gorgeous diamond. It sparkled in the sunlight streaming through the windows and he pulled it from the box and took her right hand, "This one?"

Charly nodded. "That way I can feel it."

Sam smiled and slid the ring onto her finger, then kissed her fingers. Once he'd finished, he kissed the fingers of her left hand too, then stood and turned to the kitchen.

"She said yes!"

Her RAPTOR friends, his PD friends, all of them came pouring from the kitchen and hall in a chorus of congratulations.

42

Charly sat at the conference room table in the RAPTOR compound. Today Piper, Caiden, and Creed were getting ready to leave for Vegas and final preparations were being made. They had a team meeting to discuss possible issues and to get the stand-by team, Diego and Falcon, up to speed in case there were issues.

She looked at her teammates sitting around the table and smiled. A few days ago they'd all helped her and Sam celebrate their engagement; today they were all business.

Emmy stood at the head of the table, "So, what we have is a pretty good plan. Piper, Caiden, and Creed, you'll go to Lucifer's Den, to see if you can meet a few of the team members and get to know them. Hopefully, you'll get invited to an after-party and try to meet up with more of them. Make friends. Let's get inside and see what we can find out. Jerard is in jail and will be for a long time. But if he does get out, he hasn't seen any of you. Which is why Charly and Falcon can't join you. Questions?"

Heads shook and no one had anything further to add.

Emmy continued. "One more thing. Hadleigh Keach is taking on a new position within RAPTOR. The agency has acknowledged her years of service in social work and the work she did helping to ferret out Marco48 and agreed that she'll now be able to act as a social worker within RAPTOR. Her job will be to follow up with the kids we locate and save so we don't have a situation like we did with Olive and Haylie. They won't fall through the cracks of an over-worked system if we're able to take on their follow-up care and checks through our own system. The Agency will pay for Hadleigh's services through funds earmarked for social services which helps all of us. But, I'm also excited to announce a couple of new updates and an addition to our team.

"Since the Agency has hired us, we've made more money than I thought possible at this early stage in our business. We've worked with them to hire a fulltime pilot, who will be on call with us twenty-four-seven. Her name is Teresa and she's on her way here now. She currently has a home in Florida and will divide her time between here and there. I'll introduce you to her when she gets here. With the addition of Teresa, we needed something for her to fly, and we've managed to purchase a plane that seats only eight at a time, but we don't all go together on missions anyway, so it'll work nicely for whatever we need. Just like GHOST helped us out at the beginning and when we needed a plane, Teresa, and Gavin; GHOST's pilot, will work together to support both organizations. So if one of them is flying or long-distance at a location, the other will be available to us."

"Woo, that's fantastic!" Donovan cheered.

Others cheered and clapped.

"Amazing," exclaimed Deacon.

Emmy smiled and nodded. Charly waited for the cheers to subside.

"Emmy, thank you so much for setting up RAPTOR and all you've done for this organization and these kids we're saving."

Emmy nodded. "Thank you, Charly, and all of you, for working so hard to make us a success. If the kids aren't saved, we aren't doing our job. And, I'll tell you, I'm still working to hunt down Sergeant Dildo's contacts. I will never forget what he was willing to do." Sergeant Dildo, or actually, Dillano, was their Sergeant during Operation Live Again. He'd been willing to let Olive and two other children be sold off so he could make a buck, and none of them would ever forget that.

"I'll help you, Emmy." Charly added.

"I'll take your help. Creed has been helping me as well."

"I'll help too," said Diego.

"Me too," said another.

Emmy smiled at the group of amazing people. "You all may be called on from time to time to help me. It'll be my main mission to stop that asshole. And then I'll be able to bring Dildo down too."

Emmy picked up her file and looked at Charly. "Don't you have a wedding to plan?"

"Yes ma'am. But nothing super lavish or fancy. Just something nice."

"Let me know if you need any help, Charly."

"Thanks, Emmy."

Charly walked around the table to Piper and hugged her tight.

"You be careful out there, Pipes. Don't get all brave and do something crazy. I need my maid of honor for my wedding."

Piper hugged her back. "I'll be here for certain. You just keep that big stud of yours happy and healthy till I get back."

Charly laughed, "I'm not the one who almost set the house on fire."

Piper laughed. "I'm sorry, I shouldn't laugh, but that's funny. If that's how Sam cooks, what on earth will happen if you try?"

Charly held her hands up in front of her and shook her head. "I know my limits."

"Okay, Charly, I've gotta go and make some last-minute arrangements. I'll be chatting daily with you and on the comm units. Love you."

"Love you too, Pipes."

Creed grinned and with his voice trying to mimic a female voice said, "I love you too, Charly."

Charly laughed. "Shut up, Creed. Now you make sure Piper doesn't do anything crazy. Put those bastards away and get home."

Creed saluted. "We'll do that for certain. See you Charly."

Caiden waved as he walked out the door and Charly waved back. It was weird, when it was her going on a mission, she wasn't nervous at all or thinking maudlin thoughts, but watching her teammates go out the door made her stomach a bit queasy.

When Sam got home, the stereo was playing country music and Charly was singing along from the kitchen. Something smelled fantastic and his stomach growled.

He hung his jacket in the laundry room, just off the door to the garage, and walked around the corner to see Charly arranging food on plates. Two drinks were made and sitting on the counter and she looked fantastic in a pair of short denim shorts, her spectacular legs lightly tanned and shapely.

He walked up behind her and wrapped his arms around her waist and pulled her back into his body.

"Hi handsome. How was your day?"

"Fantastic, how was yours?"

"It was pretty good. Sheldon made meatloaf today. And, he sent along baked potatoes, corn, and his famous coleslaw."

"It smells fantastic." He kissed the top of her head. "But not as good as you."

She turned in his arms. "Perfect response."

He bent and kissed her lips, molding his to hers felt so right. He bent at the knees and lifted her, and loved it when her legs instantly circled his waist.

"Damn, I love you." He managed between kisses.

She teased, "Eat first or sex first?"

His stomach growled then and she giggled. "Eat first."

He kissed her again and let her slide down his body. He was so close to telling his stomach to suck it up, but before he could make that statement, Charly had their plates on the table and reached across the counter for the drinks. He enjoyed watching her for just a moment and decided to inhale his food so he could make love to his future wife. He couldn't wait to stop calling her his *future* wife.

As he sat, she smiled and tapped her glass to his.

She smiled at him and his heart swelled. "I think I'd like a country wedding. What do you think?"

"What does a country wedding look like?"

"Well, there's a barn outside of town where they have weddings and things. The inside is decorated really cool, they have twinkle lights hung from the beams in the barn, chairs are set up for the ceremony, then afterwards, they set up tables and the food is catered in. What do you think, wanna get married in a barn?"

He laughed. "Yeah, I think I do."

Her smile was dazzling and he felt fantastic knowing he made her happy. Wasn't that just the thing? It made him happy to make her happy. Life was funny.

They finished their meal, but before the dishes were cleared, he walked up behind her and kissed her ear. His hands roamed around to her fantastic breasts and he enjoyed how they felt as he squeezed them in his hands. He pushed himself into her behind, enjoying the feel of her ass as it added pressure to his quickly growing cock.

He pinned her to the table with his hips and his hands reached down and pulled her cute little t-shirt top over her head. He flicked the clasp of her bra and pulled it from her arms. Charly giggled.

He leaned over her, now able to hold her bare breasts in his hands, and whispered in her ear. "Now this feels fantastic."

Her head lay back against his shoulder, her ass wriggled against him and his cock thickened again. He pulled back briefly and unsnapped her cute little shorts, then unzipped them and tugged on them until they slipped over her hips. She kicked at them as they hit the floor and he took that time to undo his own pants and let them fall to his ankles. He kicked them away and bent his knees and straightened to run his cock in the seam of her ass. She moaned slightly and he did it again.

He put his forefinger up to her lips and she sucked it into her mouth, sucking and swiping her tongue around it. He pulled it from her mouth and pulled her slightly away from the table and circled her clit. The moan that escaped her lips told him he hit that spot she so loved him to hit and he continued to circle around her clit, then slowly slid his finger down and slipped it inside of her pussy. She widened her stance at the table and he slid his finger back up to her clit, circling her a few more times.

"Sam." She whispered.

He pulled back and positioned his cock at her entrance, then brought his hand back around to Charly's clit and slowly entered her. Oh the feeling. He loved how tightly she hugged his cock. He pushed all the way in then pulled out. It wasn't the most comfortable position, he needed to squat low to manage his movements, but it was so worth it. His hand roved over the smooth skin of her ass as he pulled out and pushed himself back in. He rubbed her back, her sexy, smooth back and pulled out and pushed back in. His finger continued to circle her clit and she panted.

He pulled out and pushed back in, faster and faster, his need building quickly hoping to hell hers was too.

"Charly." He groaned.

"Yes."

"Now?"

In and out, in and out.

"Yes."

In and out. Charly moaned, her body jerked as she orgasmed and he pulled out and pushed back in. His orgasm rolled over him, his body jerked as he released himself inside her.

"Charly. My God, Charly."

She sighed. "Yeah."

A loud knock on the door startled him and Charly squealed. "Oh my God, whose here?"

They quickly pulled themselves together and redressed. Sam bent and kissed her lips quickly. "I love you."

"I love you too."

He walked to the door and Charly picked up the dishes and walked them to the sink.

Sam opened the door to his parents standing on the doorstep, big smiles on their faces.

"Surprise." They both cheered.

His face flamed hot and red; of course they had no way of knowing what had just happened on the dinner table, but, well, you know.

Sam bent down and scooped his mom up into an embrace, then shook his dad's hand. Charly came into the room from the kitchen, her face just as red as his felt.

Sam walked over to her and smiled, then kissed her lightly and pulled her forward to meet his parents.

"Charly, meet my parents Harvey and Rebecca."

His mom stepped forward and engulfed Charly in a motherly squeeze, and his dad grinned ear to ear as he hugged her close.

"It's such a pleasure to meet you Charly. Sam has told us so much about you."

"Thank you, it's nice to meet you too. Sam talks about both of you quite a bit too. All good."

Charly's phone rang and she stepped back to look at the read-out. "It's Piper, I have to take this. I'm sorry."

Sam nodded. "Go ahead babe, I'll get Mom and Dad settled in."

Charly tapped her phone and waved to his parents as she went to the bedroom. "Hey, Pipes."

C harly sat on the edge of the bed and listened as Piper rattled out her dilemma.

"Charly, I have a sudden bout of nerves. In two days, we're heading to the nightclub and just seeing some of the women I'm seeing on the internet at the nightclub's website, have me feeling like I'll stick out like a sore thumb."

"No you won't, Pipes. You pull your shoulders back, stand tall, and walk in there like you mean it. Plus, with your back, you almost always walk like that anyway, so you're already there. Do your hair up and remember that you're trying to look wealthy."

Piper chuckled. "Okay."

"Pipes, Sam's parents just showed up without letting us know and I'm nervous as shit."

"What? Are you kidding? You're as badass as they come. And, they'll love you."

Charly took a deep breath. "Thanks, Pipes. Okay, I've got to get going and meet them properly. I'm here for you."

"Okay. Love you."

Charly tapped her phone again and took a deep breath. She pocketed her phone and walked out to the living room where Sam and his parents sat visiting. She smiled when she entered the room, Sam held out his hand to her and she walked over and sat next to him on the love seat.

"Everything alright?"

"Yes. She's just nervous." Sam's parents smiled reassuringly and she felt she needed to explain a bit. "I work for an organization who employs only wounded veterans." She held up her left arm. "We rescue trafficked children." That was the PG version. "I was compromised during our last mission, so my friend Piper, who hasn't gone out in the field in a couple of years, is filling in for me. I just did a quick pep talk."

Sam's mom sat forward. "So when you say you've been compromised, what does that mean?"

Charly smiled her best smile. "It means the traffickers we're trying to bring down have seen me. So, I can't go there. They've also seen a couple of my co-workers, so another team is out there now. I'll be back at headquarters helping in other ways. Research and reconnaissance from satellite."

Sam's dad looked at Sam, who was staring at Charly. She smiled at Sam; his admiration of her was all on display. "That sounds dangerous."

Sam leaned forward and took Charly's hand in his. "It can be. But Charly and her team are good, Dad. Impressively good." He kissed her fingers and she melted.

"Thank you."

Sam's mom smiled. "Shall we make wedding plans then?"

***

Click below to read what happens during the planning and attend the wedding of Charly and Sam.

To attend the wedding go here: https://www.pjfiala.com/books/CCEpilogue

***

Piper and crew are headed to the sensational and nefarious Las Vegas to continue tracking traffickers. All is not what it seems with the Las Vegas Sinners. And Piper is heading out to the field for the first time as a RAPTOR operative. It's a nail-biter! https://www.pjfiala.com/books/promising-piper/

ALSO BY PJ FIALA

Click here to see a list of all of my books with the blurbs.

Contemporary Romance
Rolling Thunder Series

Moving to Love, Book 1

Moving to Hope, Book 2

Moving to Forever, Book 3

Moving to Desire, Book 4

Moving to You, Book 5

Moving Home, Book 6

Moving On, Book 7

Rolling Thunder Boxset, Books 1-4

Military Romantic Suspense
Second Chances Series

Designing Samantha's Love, Book 1

Securing Kiera's Love, Book 2

Second Chances Boxset - Duet

Bluegrass Security Series

Heart Thief, Book One

Finish Line, Book Two

Lethal Love, Book Three

Bluegrass Security Boxset, Books 1-3

Big 3 Security

Ford: Finding His Fire Book One

Lincoln: Finding His Mark Book Two

Dodge: Finding His Jewel Book Three

Rory: Finding His Match Book Four

Big 3 Security Boxset, Books 1-4

GHOST

Defending Keirnan, GHOST Book One

Defending Sophie, GHOST Book Two

Defending Roxanne, GHOST Book Three

Defending Yvette, GHOST Book Four

Defending Bridget, GHOST Book Five

Defending Isabella, GHOST Book Six

RAPTOR

Saving Shelby, RAPTOR Book One

Holding Hadleigh, RAPTOR Book Two

Craving Charlesia, RAPTOR Book Three

Promising Piper, RAPTOR Book Four

Missing Mia, RAPTOR Book Five

Believing Becca, RAPTOR Book Six

Keeping Kori, RAPTOR Book Seven

Healing Hope, RAPTOR Book Eight

Engaging Emersyn, RAPTOR Book Nine

MEET PJ

Writing has been a desire my whole life. Once I found the courage to write, life changed for me in the most profound way. Bringing stories to readers that I'd enjoy reading and creating characters that are flawed, but lovable is such a joy.

When not writing, I'm with my family doing something fun. My husband, Gene, and I are bikers and enjoy riding to new locations, meeting new people and generally enjoying this fabulous country we live in.

I come from a family of veterans. My grandfather, father, brother, two sons, and one daughter-in-law are all veterans. Needless to say, I am proud to be an American and proud of the service my amazing family has given.

My online home is https://www.pjfiala.com.
You can connect with me on Facebook at https://www.
facebook.com/PJFiala1,

and
Instagram at https://www.Instagram.com/PJFiala.
If you prefer to email, go ahead, I'll respond -
pjfiala@pjfiala.com.

Made in the USA
Monee, IL
23 September 2022